NIGHTMARE HALL

The Silent Scream

NON-STOP THRILLS

NIGHTMARE HALL

The Silent Scream

DIANE HOH

SCHOLASTIC INC.

New York   Toronto   London   Auckland   Sydney
Mexico City   New Delhi   Hong Kong   Buenos Aires

No part of this publication may be reproduced in whole or in part, or stored in a retrieval system, or transmitted in any form or by any means, electronic, mechanical, photocopying, recording, or otherwise, without written permission of the publisher. For information regarding permission, write to Scholastic Inc., Attention: Permissions Department, 557 Broadway, New York, NY 10012.

ISBN 0-590-46014-5

12 11 10 9 8 7 6 5 4 3 2 1   4 5 6 7 8 9/0

Printed in the U.S.A.   01

First Point Thriller printing, September 2004

NIGHTMARE HALL

The Silent Scream

Prologue

The housemother who found Giselle Mc-
Kendrick hanging from the brass light fixture
in her bedroom didn't scream. When she entered the room on the second floor of Nightingale Hall, an off-campus dormitory at Salem
University, and found Giselle suspended, swaying gently above the shiny hardwood floor, Isobel Coates's mouth opened in horror, but she
made no sound.

For several minutes, the only sound in the
bright and sunny room came from the birds
outside, screeching in the huge oak trees shad-
owing the tall, skinny, old brick house. Sheer
white curtains at the narrow windows moved
gently, ghostlike, stirred by a warm June
breeze.

As Mrs. Coates's wrinkled, brown-spotted
hands rushed to cover her mouth, the neatly
folded stack of white linens she was carrying

1

hit the polished floor with a soft slap. "Oh," she whispered, "oh, oh, oh . . ."

Young, pretty Giselle McKendrick's body was a lazy pendulum swinging from the light fixture. She was wearing white shorts and a bright yellow halter top because of the rare, early June intense heat wave. But that heat was oddly absent in the small, square space. Giselle's bedroom was icily cold.

The girl's bare, tanned legs dangled lifelessly. Her head hung at a harsh angle. Her blue eyes stared blindly at the wall, and her mouth was frozen open in a voiceless scream. Her curly blonde hair brushed against her broken neck as she swayed back and forth, back and forth . . .

A length of rope, one end fastened firmly around the stem of the old-fashioned light fixture, encircled Giselle's slender throat.

Mrs. Coates, her mouth still hidden behind her hands, began moving slowly backward, murmuring, "No, no, no . . ."

The other five students living in the rooming house came home that afternoon to find Giselle's room unoccupied, the purple spread neatly pulled up over the bed, the white curtains still stirring gently. The news of their friend's death shocked each of them into stupified silence. They stumbled about the house, crying, glassy-eyed with disbelief.

Although the rest of the house shimmered with stultifying heat, that one small space on the second floor remained bone-chillingly cold, as if wrapped in an icy December wind.

Giselle's housemates left for summer vacation in somber silence. According to a small, unobtrusive article in the local newspaper shortly before they left Nightingale Hall, the official verdict on Giselle's death was "apparent suicide." It seemed that Giselle McKendrick had chosen to stop living, and no one who knew her understood why.

It was beyond understanding.

The housemates vowed never to return to Nightingale Hall. How could they? They would live instead in one of the on-campus dorms, away from painful reminders of their friend.

They emptied closets and drawers and desks and then, loaded down with suitcases, trunks, and backpacks, left Nightingale Hall behind forever. There were no backward glances as they made their way down the gravel driveway that snaked up over the hill and curved along the front of the house. A glance over the shoulder might serve as an unpleasant reminder that six, not five, students had taken up residence in the three-storied brick dormitory nine months earlier. That seemed, now, like a lifetime ago.

When the last student had gone, Mrs. Coates draped the living room, dining room, and library furniture with heavy cloths and then packed her own suitcase. She was spending the summer at the beach. Perhaps, away from the dorm and its empty rooms, she could forget the terrible sight of that lovely young girl's body swinging from the ceiling in the small, sunny bedroom.

As the housemother's taxi pulled away on a warm June evening, the empty dorm seemed to settle further into its grassy knoll overlooking the campus. Huge, giant-limbed oak trees shading the house made its dark red brick look almost black. The floor-to-ceiling windows facing the wide front porch were completely shuttered, as if the house had closed its eyes to sleep. Even the birds had left, taking their songs with them. An eerie silence fell over the hill.

Lost in shadow and deepening twilight, the house settled into the hillside to wait.

All summer long, it waited . . .

Chapter 1

Jessica Vogt leaned forward, her navy-blue eyes staring out the bus window. She wanted to take in every detail of the town of Twin Falls where she would be spending the next four years of her life. The main street, Pennsylvania Avenue, crowded with traffic now as other college students like herself arrived in town, was flanked on one side by a slowly meandering river, on the other side by shops and restaurants, a red brick post office, several bank buildings. Shoppers accustomed to the annual onslaught of young people ignored the long line of cars and buses snaking its way through the center of town and went about their business.

The bus passed slowly through the center of town, advancing past a stone bridge on the left spanning the river, and a beautiful row of lavish white and brick homes on the right, facing the water. A huge stone church took up one whole block, its spire rising some distance above the medium-sized community. Tall, full trees lined the avenue in front of the church. A larger section of more modest homes followed, and then, at the edge of town, a large, sprawling shopping mall.

Jess could already see the rooftops of the university buildings some distance ahead, just beyond the town. She settled back in her seat. It was a pretty town, not unlike her own hometown. Peaceful, quiet . . . and it had a mall. She smiled. What would life be like without a mall?

The bus let her off just a block from Nightingale Hall, the off-campus dorm where she would be living.

When it had gone, she walked up the block, and paused at the bottom of the curving gravelled driveway that led up the slope to the house. Hands in the pockets of her khaki shorts, a set of cheap brown luggage resting beside her sandalled feet, she grimaced in dismay as her eyes focused on the building destined to be her home from September to June. It wasn't very inviting.

"Great place to film a horror movie," she murmured, running a hand through her short, glossy black hair. Shifting slightly, she kept her gaze on the house.

It was tall and narrow, three stories of brick so deep a red and so shaded by massive oaks it looked charcoal. Two of the dark green shutters flanking the tall, skinny windows were hanging crookedly and the wide, wooden porch sagged just enough to make the house look a little drunk. A metal fire escape traveled from the ground up to the third story along the left-hand side.

In case we ever need an escape route, Jess thought.

The house stood, tired and worn, at the top of the slope, overlooking the hill and the highway with, Jess had to admit, a certain kind of dignity in spite of its shabbiness.

It's seen better days, she thought with conviction. It must have been beautiful once.

The lawn had recently been mowed, filling the air with the smell of fresh-cut grass, and the squat green shrubbery flanking the wide front porch was thick with round, red berries.

"Pretty grim, huh?" a deep voice behind Jess asked. "Looks a little like Tara, *after* the Civil War." A chuckle followed the comment. "Your name wouldn't by any chance be Scarlett, would it?"

Jess turned around. The boy who stood behind her was taller than her own five feet six inches. His shoulder-length straight, dark hair was tied back in a careless ponytail. He was wearing faded denim cutoffs and a white T-shirt. A huge, worn black leather camera case was slung over one shoulder.

"You *have* read *Gone With the Wind*, haven't you?" he asked, smiling. "Or at least seen the movie?"

Jess nodded. If his nose hadn't had a slight hook to it, he would have been *too* good-looking. Boys who were too good-looking seemed to think the world owed them something. "Of course I've read it. It happens to be one of my favorites. And you're right about the house. It's pretty grim. But," shrugging her thin shoulders, "it's cheaper than on-campus dorms, so I guess we shouldn't expect too much."

Extending a hand, he said, "Ian Banion." He grinned as they shook hands. "Who cares what the place looks like? I came for the fishing. I checked this place out last spring. There's a great stream out back." Another sheepish grin. "But I'm also here because it's cheaper." Glancing up the hill, he added, "Anyway, you've got to admit this place looks more interesting than those boring stone dorms on campus."

Jess cocked an eyebrow. Interesting? Maybe. "It's probably a lot nicer on the inside."

Ian looked dubious. "I wouldn't count on it. C'mon, let's check it out."

They were halfway up the hill when someone shouting behind them brought them to a halt. Turning in tandem, they found another boy hurrying to catch up to them. "Wait up!" he called. "I'm not going into that mausoleum by myself. Could be dangerous." He was carrying two very expensive-looking leather bags.

"Oh, come on," Jess said. "I'll bet it was gorgeous once upon a time. I think it's those trees . . . they keep the sun from lighting up the place."

The newcomer was not as tall as Ian, but he had broader shoulders and a deeper tan. His wheat-colored hair had been blow-dried and moussed perfectly in place. His white knit shirt looked expensive, as did the perfectly creased navy blue slacks he was wearing. His features were even, nearly perfect. The sort of face, Jess thought, that graces magazine covers. His arrogant smile told her he thought the same thing.

If he had money, and he certainly looked as if he did, what was he doing at Nightingale Hall?

He fixed warm brown eyes on Jess and answered her unspoken question. "I picked an off-campus place because I figured the rules would be a cinch to break, but now I see that fate sent me here. Hello, *gorgeous*! Jon Shea, here."

Jess's immediate reaction was, Spare me! Jon Shea was one of *those*: *too* good-looking. Probably couldn't function for more than five minutes without a mirror handy. He most likely found the "chase" after a girl the most exciting part of any relationship. Once the "quarry" had been caught, he probably lost interest. She'd bet the streets of his hometown were paved with broken hearts.

"Jessica Vogt," she said, her voice cool. "And this is Ian Banion."

"So," Jon said cheerfully, "we're all going to be residents of Nightmare Hall?"

Jessica laughed. "Oh, quit exaggerating. It's not *that* bad."

Two girls and another boy, surrounded by their baggage, were already seated on the floor of the porch when Jess arrived with Ian and Jon.

One girl jumped to her feet. She was tall and broad-shouldered, with tanned sturdy legs in bright green shorts. Her hair was short and yellow, with a slight greenish tinge to it.

A swimmer, Jess decided. That hair had been overdosed with chlorine.

"Hi," the girl said with a friendly smile, "I'm Linda Carlyle. Is one of you, I hope, the new monitor? Because if you are, you might have a key, and I'm dying to get inside for a nice, cool drink of water. I'm so parched my throat feels like sandpaper, and the door seems to be locked."

"I'm the monitor," Jess answered, moving forward. She had taken the job in return for a break in her tuition. "And you're in luck. Mrs. Coates mailed me a key. We can all go inside. Isn't she here?"

Linda shook her head. "No one answered when I knocked. I tried the bell, too, but it doesn't work."

"Figures," Jon remarked drily. "This place could use a live-in handyman."

"Somebody call me?" a voice asked as a young man in white overalls and T-shirt came around the corner of the house. He was short and stocky, with thick, curly black hair. His well-muscled arms were sunburned, as were his cheeks and neck. "Am I needed here?"

"Are you kidding?" Jon asked. "Take a good look around. Those shutters are hanging at half-mast and the porch is listing to starboard and . . ."

The young man in overalls smiled coldly. "Go boating a lot, do you?" The smile told Jess he had already pegged Jon as a "rich boy." "Relax. It'll get done. I've been working inside, getting the rooms ready. I'm Trucker Swopes. And you are . . . ?"

"Jon Shea. This is Jessica Vogt and Ian . . . sorry, I forgot the last name."

"Banion. I can't introduce the others because we haven't met yet. We just arrived."

"I'll help," the blond swimmer volunteered. "I'm Linda Carlyle, and this is Cath Devon, and over here is Milo Keith." She smiled down at Milo. "They're freshmen, too."

Jess looked with interest at the pair as Trucker acknowledged the introductions by shaking everyone's hand. Cath Devon was tiny, and would have been pretty if she hadn't looked so tense and anxious. She had very pale skin and a mass of dark, curly hair that spilled across her shoulders and threatened to overwhelm her. She was dressed in preppy clothes: a blue plaid, pleated skirt and a blue crew-neck sweater, but the heat didn't seem to be bothering her at all.

She should be melting in that outfit, Jess thought, but she looks as cool as April rain. Still, there was something about her mouth . . . the jaws were clenched too tightly. And didn't that look like fear in those dark eyes?

Well, weren't they all a little scared? Leaving home for the first time could do that.

Milo Keith was very tall and very thin. His hair was long and needed both combing and trimming, as did the tangle of beard hiding his chin. His eyes were a brilliant blue behind wire-rimmed glasses.

Giving Trucker, Jess, and Jon no more than a polite nod, Milo returned to the book he'd been reading, positioned on his crisscrossed legs.

"Where is Mrs. Coates?" Jess asked Trucker as she moved toward the big, wooden front door. She fumbled in her backpack for the key.

"She went to town," Trucker told her. "Said if you didn't have your key with you, I was to let you in. You got it?"

Jess unearthed the key and nodded.

"Well, go ahead then," he said, smiling slightly. "No sense standing around out here.

I've got to get back to work. You need anything, give me a holler."

"Thanks." The picture of herself "hollering" for help wasn't an appealing one, but it was nice to know that if she did, someone would come. She inserted the key into the lock and turned the fat, brass doorknob.

And then, although she couldn't have explained why, instead of entering first, which would have been logical since she was the one who had opened the door, she stood back and urged the others in ahead of her.

I'm just being polite, she told herself as they marched inside. I'm letting them go in first because my mother raised me properly and I'm extremely well-mannered.

"What's the matter?" Trucker asked, looking up at her thoughtfully from the wide stone steps he was sweeping. "Scared?"

And it occurred to her that she was.

Chapter 2

Scolding herself for being silly, Jess moved on inside the house, closing the heavy door behind her.

As she followed the others from living room to library, dining room, and kitchen, Jess's first impression was of space. The rooms were large and contained massive pieces of old, dark furniture. The high ceilings made her feel dwarfed.

"I feel like the Incredible Shrinking Freshman," she told Linda, who giggled nervously as they entered the library with its floor-to-ceiling bookshelves. "Our entire apartment back home would easily fit into this room. No wonder this place is used as a dorm."

Her second impression was of darkness and gloom. Although the house was immaculate, the hardwood floors smooth and shiny with polish, every window was completely draped with heavy fabrics: gold in the dining room, maroon in the living room and library. Hardly any natural light crept in. The first floor of Nightingale Hall was as dark as a cave.

"I hope those drapes open," Jess said, frowning at the windows. She liked sunshine and light. Adjusting to this gloomy old place would be hard.

Cath pursed her lips disapprovingly at Jess's comment. "I don't think we should touch the drapes. Not until Mrs. Coates gets here."

She's nervous, Jess thought. She's afraid of getting into trouble. Hasn't she ever been in trouble before? Never got caught cutting a class or staying out too late or forgetting a school assignment? Weird.

"Relax," Jess said, "I won't touch the drapes, I promise. Not yet, anyway. We'll have to convince our housemother that we need lots of light or we'll get all pale and shriveled, like dying plants."

Ian grinned at her. "I can't picture *you* all pale and shriveled."

It sounded like a compliment. He probably expected a grateful smile in return.

Well, why not? It wasn't as if she had been deluged with compliments all summer. She'd been too busy working to pay any attention to the boys who came into the mall. College was incredibly expensive and her scholarship didn't cover everything.

But she'd *made* enough money and now she was *here*, so if someone was willing to compliment her, she was more than willing to listen.

She smiled back at Ian.

"Nice smile," he said as they entered the long, narrow kitchen situated at the rear of the house.

The room was large, spotlessly clean and, thanks to a half-wall of windows above the sink and dishwasher, brighter than the rest of the house. The windows overlooked the back slope leading down into a thick, wooded area and, Ian told her, the stream.

Leaving the kitchen, they all trooped upstairs to check out their rooms.

Jess was pleasantly surprised by hers. This isn't half-bad, she thought as she swung open the door bearing a small name-tag reading *JESSICA VOGT*. She stood in the doorway, smiling with pleasure. The room was small, but bright and sunny. The walls were papered in a dainty lilac-flowered print, the bed covered with a vivid purple spread, topped with a folded, flowered quilt. A pretty wooden desk and chair sat between a pair of tall, narrow windows framed by sheer white curtains. A squat, fat chest of drawers of dark wood sat along one wall, waiting for Jess's clothing.

The room smelled of lemon, and of fresh air, wafting in through the open windows.

"This is really pretty," she murmured to herself, "and it's all *mine*!" She had never had a room of her own before.

But as she stepped across the threshold, a suitcase weighing down each hand, she was met by a wave of air so cold it took her breath away. The unexpected chill wrapped itself around her, penetrating her thin T-shirt, her shorts, and heading straight for her bones.

Jess gasped in shock. She felt as if she'd been doused with ice water.

She took an involuntary step backward. The air in the hall was warm. Puzzled, she basked in the welcome warmth for only a minute. Then, thinking she must have imagined the chill, she re-entered the room.

But the chill was still there. She hadn't imagined it.

She stayed where she was, a look of confusion on her face. Where was that cool air coming from? The windows were open, but she knew the air outside wasn't cold. Unless a sudden cold front had moved in.

Dropping the suitcases and hugging herself for warmth, Jess moved to one of the open windows and thrust a bare arm forward. The air that touched her skin was still mild, caressing it with no hint of chill.

But inside her room . . .

She turned again to face her new home. She took a step away from the window, then another . . .

There was nothing imaginary about the cool air that descended upon her the moment she left the window. With her arms still wrapped around her chest, she sat down on the bed.

Maybe there was something about old houses . . . isolated pockets of cold air? She could ask Trucker. He might know. Or . . . hadn't there been a fireplace in the living room? The chimney should be right about . . . Jess stood up, pacing off steps . . . right about here! Inside her closet. Probably right behind her closet wall. If the chimney went all the way down to a cellar, what she was feeling was probably cold cellar air leaking into her room from loose chimney bricks.

Jess went back to the bed, shrugging. So she'd wear sweaters. The room was too pretty, and the privacy, after sharing a room with two sisters, was too welcome to be upset over a little thing like a slight chill in the air. If she'd moved into a dorm on campus, she would have had to share.

When she had finished unpacking, Jess wandered down the dark, narrow hall to see how her new housemates were doing.

Chapter 3

The doors to all the rooms were standing open. Cath was unpacking what seemed to Jess an endless supply of sweaters, Linda had already appropriated one of the two bathrooms, and Jon, fresh from a shower, was primping in front of his dresser mirror.

He won't be here long, Jess thought, watching with amusement as Jon coaxed a wheat-colored wave into place on his forehead. He'll pledge a fraternity and move into a frat house on campus. Maybe somebody with a little more depth than a bed sheet will take his place.

"I was thinking about a little get-acquainted party on the porch tonight," she suggested when he turned and saw her standing in the doorway. "Interested?" She was sure he'd dismiss it as being dull.

He surprised her by agreeing enthusiastically. "Cath'll be there, right?" he asked.

Jess grinned. So, he'd already switched his attention from Jess to Cath. No surprise there. The petite type with tons of hair would appeal to him. But would *he* appeal to Cath? She seemed so . . . withdrawn. Not at all outgoing like Jon.

It would be interesting to see what, if anything, developed between them.

Ian, a towel over his shoulder, approached from the opposite end of the hall.

"How's your room?" Jess asked.

He shrugged. "A room's a room. Four walls, a ceiling . . . what more could anyone ask for?" He grinned. She noticed a tiny space between his upper front teeth, and thought it was cute. "I told you, I'm just here for the fishing."

"So, are you fishing tonight, or do you feel up to a little party on the front porch? We could talk a little bit about how things should work around here, and get to know each other. What do you think?"

"I think, fine. Anyone else interested?"

"Just Jon, so far. I haven't checked with the others yet. I was just about to see if I could drag Linda out of the bathroom."

Linda was delighted with the idea of a porch party. "A party already? Great! I can find out more about Milo. Don't you think he's really cute?"

Jess agreed that Milo was "really cute" but privately thought that "finding out more about Milo" would be more challenging to Linda-the-swimmer than trying to take seven gold medals in the Olympics. The way he'd dived back into his book after their introductions this afternoon told her he was probably either painfully shy or seriously antisocial, or a combination of both.

"What'll we eat?" Linda asked.

"Pizza, what else?" Jess answered. She began leafing through the telephone book on the small table in the upstairs hall, which also held a phone. "There has to be a pizza place that delivers. It's un-American not to have at least one."

The town of Twin Falls wasn't un-American. It had several pizza restaurants that delivered and, Jess noticed as she flicked through the telephone book, a bowling alley, a movie theater, and half a dozen restaurants that, judging by the upbeat ads in the yellow pages, catered to the college crowd. One in particular, a diner called Burgers Etc. had a picture of the university's administration building in its ad.

That done, Jess went back downstairs to await the arrival of their housemother and make sure their get-acquainted party was okay with her.

Mrs. Coates, an elderly woman with graying hair, her ample girth enveloped in a worn but garish green-and-orange print dress, had no objection to the party. "Might as well get to know each other right off the bat. My kids always end up being good friends. Hate to leave each other when summer comes."

Her round, wrinkled face suddenly clouded over, as if a painful memory had just crossed her mind. She turned away from Jess. "Go ahead and have your party," she said over her shoulder. "Long as you clean up any mess."

"We will." Mrs. Coates, Jess decided as she left the kitchen, must miss the kids who moved on after graduation. That would explain the sudden sadness in her face.

The party got off to a good start. The evening was warm, almost balmy, and it was quiet and peaceful on the hill. An intermittent hum sounded from the highway below as an occasional car passed, but the birds had quieted down for the night. Jess had borrowed a dozen fat, stubby candles from Mrs. Coates and stuck them in clay flowerpots Trucker had brought from the potting shed behind the house. They were scattered about the large porch, the candle glow providing a soft, pale illumination.

The pizza wasn't very good, but no one seemed to care. They talked about why they had chosen Nightingale Hall over on-campus dorms. Finances had decided everyone but Jon and Cath. Linda and Ian had athletic scholarships that failed to cover room and board, Linda's for swimming, Ian's for baseball.

"It would be lots more convenient living on campus," Linda admitted, wiping tomato sauce from her mouth with a paper napkin. "I'd be closer to the pool. But my folks couldn't swing the room and board on campus. So here I am!" She beamed at Milo, who ignored her.

But his expression brightened when Ian and Trucker mentioned the stream in the woods behind the house. "No kidding? That's great! I've written some of my best poetry while I was sitting on a riverbank, fishing." He smiled at Ian, and Jess was surprised at how Milo's thin, pale face warmed when he smiled. "Man," Milo added, "you've made my day!"

"Well, I'm just glad you're happy," Cath said sourly. "Personally, I *hate* old houses. They give me the creeps." She pushed a thick clump of wiry black hair behind one ear. "I'm here because my parents decided living off-campus would be less distracting." She made a face of distaste. "Meaning I wouldn't have any *fun*. Not that I'd know fun if it walked up and bit me." Her voice took on a cool, haughty tone as she quoted: " 'The object of education is to educate, not to entertain.' " She laughed harshly. "*That* is my father speaking, and trust me, he meant every word of it. If I hadn't known that before I saw this place, I certainly knew it when he dropped me off this afternoon."

"Oh, I *love* old houses," Linda gushed. "That's why I'm planning to major in design. I want to remodel old houses, reclaim them. They have so much history."

"Yeah," Ian said, his voice grim, "sometimes *too* much. And not always good, either."

Jess, in the process of lifting the last soggy slice of pizza from the flat cardboard box on the porch floor, looked up. "What's *that* supposed to mean? Do you know something about old houses that we don't?"

The highway hum had ended. The hill lay in silence. Except for the pale glow of the flickering candles, darkness shrouded the house, erasing the rest of the world. Ian, his legs stretched out in front of him, his back against the wooden porch railing, returned Jess's gaze.

"Not *all* old houses, maybe," he said. "But *this* one definitely has a history." Then he shook his head. "Never mind. I shouldn't have said anything."

Jess shrieked, "You can't *do* that! You can't start something and not finish it. You have to tell us now. You *know* something about this place. What *is* it?"

"No, I . . ."

Jess glared. "*Tell!*"

"Well . . . it's just . . . someone died here last spring."

Cath gasped. Linda's eyes opened very wide, and Jess stared at Ian. "Died? Here?" No wonder Mrs. Coates had looked so sad.

Ian nodded reluctantly. "A girl. Giselle something. A freshman."

Jess swallowed hard. "Was she sick?"

"Um . . . no. Never mind." Ian reached for the cardboard box. "Let's start cleaning up this mess . . ."

"*Ian!* How did she die?"

"Okay, okay. But I never should have brought this up. I guess you all would have heard it on campus, though. The girl . . . she hung herself."

A shocked silence captured the porch.

"Hung herself?" Jess whispered. "Here?"

Ian nodded again. "Upstairs."

Jess sat back on her haunches, her eyes fastened on Ian's face. "Upstairs?" she barely breathed. "*Where* upstairs?"

His head down, he mumbled something.

"I can't hear you. Where?"

Ian lifted his head. "I said, isn't your room purple?"

The pizza cutter Jess had borrowed from the kitchen dropped from her hands. "Sort of. The bedspread is purple. Why?" The pizza she had just consumed suddenly felt like a fire in her stomach. Why was Ian asking about her room?

"I'm sorry, Jess," he said sincerely. "I wish I'd kept my big mouth shut. I guess I can't back up now, can I?"

"No, you can't." Her mouth was very dry. "So tell me where this . . . Giselle? . . . hung herself."

Ian's voice was very quiet, but she could hear him clearly. "The kid who brought the pizza told me a girl named Giselle committed suicide last spring in the purple room — that's what he called it. She died in her own room. The room that's yours now."

Chapter 4

Trucker emerged from the outside cellar door to find the six housemates sitting on the floor of the porch in stunned silence.

"Whoa!" he cried with a grin, "this is your idea of a party? I've seen people having more fun at funerals."

Ian flushed. "I told them about the girl who killed herself upstairs last spring. Bad move on my part."

"We would have heard about it sooner or later," Jess said quietly. "I'm glad we heard it here instead of on campus." But she didn't *look* glad. Her face was very pale.

Trucker took a seat on the top step. "I heard that girl was really popular, and smart. Not the kind of person you'd think would do something so . . ."

"So stupid?" Cath finished for him. "Maybe," she said softly, with a hint of bitterness, "she just got sick and tired of trying to please every-one. I know what that's like. If I ever got a grade lower than A, both my parents would have a heart attack." She laughed without humor. "The first simultaneous heart attack in medical history. His and Hers heart attacks, like matching bath towels."

"I don't think it was like that," Trucker dis-agreed. "Seems to me that someone said one of her parents had died. That girl's, I mean. Maybe that's why she was depressed."

The thought of a parent dying, even one who expected too much, silenced Cath. She leaned back against the porch wall and began gnawing on a fingernail. Lost in thought, she failed to notice when Jon sent her a sympathetic smile.

His handsome face registered disappoint-ment, and then annoyance that she hadn't been paying attention.

Linda's voice quavered slightly as she com-mented, "I don't understand someone giving up like that. Every swimming coach I've had always hammered into us that you never, never give up, no matter what! You keep going."

"Maybe this girl Giselle wasn't a swimmer." Jon took a healthy swig from his soda can. "Sounds like she didn't even know how to stay afloat." Then he added absentmindedly, "I wonder if she was pretty . . ."

"Jon!" Jess cried in disgust.

"I wasn't working here then," Trucker said, "but I heard she was a knockout. Drop-dead gorgeous. Long, blonde hair, blue eyes . . ."

"Geez!" Milo cried, surprising everyone, "this is supposed to be a party, not a wake! I'm not wild about parties, but I've been to a few, and one subject that never came up was suicide."

As he uttered the word "suicide," a window somewhere above them slammed shut with a violent bang.

Everyone jumped.

Jon laughed. "The house doesn't like our topic of conversation any more than Milo does."

"Maybe this place is haunted," Milo said. "I've read that people who take their own lives have restless spirits and can never find peace. They don't know where to go to find it, so they hang around the place of their death. Maybe that girl's spirit is still around here somewhere."

"Now who's being morbid?" Jess said, and Linda and Cath nodded agreement.

And although Milo smiled to imply that he

t really serious, Jess wasn't convinced.
ad certainly *sounded* serious.

Sne stood up. "I don't know about anyone else, but my party mood has disappeared along with the last of the pizza. Let's clean up this mess and call it a night, okay?"

Although Jon grumbled under his breath and Linda hung back near Milo, hoping he would notice her, the others began picking up crumpled napkins and tomato-sauced paper plates. The mood of excitement and adventure brought on by their arrival in a new place had been broken by Ian's depressing story. The party was over. Each of them took a load of trash and followed Jess into the house.

They were on their way to the kitchen when their housemother's voice called from above, "Party over?" Mrs. Coates was standing at the top of the wide, circular staircase.

"Yeah, we're beat," Jess answered. "But we'll clean up our mess."

She was never sure exactly what happened next. One minute, the elderly woman was standing at the top of the stairs in a faded green bathrobe, her graying hair festooned with pink foam-rubber rollers, and she was smiling down at them.

And the next minute, she was spiraling out into the air, her arms waving frantically, her body slamming down upon the stairs with a sickening *thunk*.

Jess screamed. She dropped the load of paper plates she was carrying. In one mass movement, the group rushed to the stairs.

Mrs. Coates hadn't fallen far. She lay sprawled awkwardly across the fourth and fifth steps from the top. Her face was twisted in pain, but she was conscious.

"My land!" she gasped as they reached her side, "how did *that* happen?"

"Don't move," Ian ordered. "We'll call an ambulance."

Cath rushed to do just that.

"No, I . . ." Mrs. Coates struggled to sit up, but gasped in pain and sank back against the step. "Oh, mercy, maybe you're right. I think it's my hip . . ."

"I don't understand," Jess whispered to Ian. "She was just *standing* there. What happened?"

"Must have tripped," Milo said, staring down at the injured woman. "I didn't see it happen, but she must have."

"Maybe she slipped on something," Linda

said, tears of sympathy pooling in her eyes. "I'll go see if there's anything in the hall. We don't want anyone else falling."

But she found nothing in the hall that might have tripped Mrs. Coates.

They waited for the ambulance to arrive. "What am I going to do about you children?" Mrs. Coates moaned. Ian had covered her with a blanket and Jess had placed a pillow behind her head in an effort to make her more comfortable. Her face was an alarming shade of gray.

Under other circumstances, they might have bristled at being called children. Milo surprised Jess by saying calmly, "We'll be fine. Not to worry."

"No . . . no, I'm responsible for you." Mrs. Coates struggled to concentrate, although it was clear to everyone watching that pain was draining her strength. "You must call my friend Madeline. Madeline Carthew. She'll come and stay with you if they keep me in the hospital." She gasped then, and fell silent.

"You won't be there that long," Jess said, hoping it was true. "We'll be fine here, really."

"Call Maddie," the housemother insisted. "The number is in the back of the telephone book. She'll come." Her eyes were closing. "Can't . . . you can't stay here alone." She was fading fast. "Promise . . . promise you'll call Maddie. Need . . . someone in charge. Promise."

Jess would have said almost anything at that point to give Mrs. Coates peace of mind. "We promise." A siren's scream approached the house. "We'll call your friend. Please don't worry."

"In the back of the telephone book," Mrs. Coates repeated. "Maddie's number."

Trucker went with Mrs. Coates and the ambulance. Jess reluctantly dialed the number of Mrs. Coates's friend, Madeline Carthew. Because she had promised.

There was no answer.

When she realized no one was going to answer, Jess hung up. I'll try again tomorrow, she told herself, and went into the kitchen. Her housemates had gathered around the small round wooden table in the center of the room. No longer brightened by daytime sunshine, the kitchen was now almost as gloomy as the rest of the house.

"I don't see why we can't fend for ourselves," Ian said when Jess reported what had happened with her phone call.

"Me, either," Milo agreed. "We're adults, right?"

Cath groaned. "Are you kidding? If my parents found out I was living in this house without a chaperon, they'd yank me out of here so fast, my hair would fall out."

If Jess hadn't been so depressed, she would have smiled. With all that hair, it would take one superhuman yank to render Cath bald.

"Who'd *tell* them?" Ian asked. "They wouldn't have to know."

"Hey, wait a minute," Jon protested. "Mrs. Coates was supposed to fix nice, home-cooked meals for us. Meat, mashed potatoes, gravy, you know, all that good stuff I'm used to. I'm a growing boy. I need nourishment."

"Why can't we all cook?" Linda suggested. "Simple stuff, like soup and sandwiches and pasta. We can take turns, or everyone can fix their own."

"I don't know," Cath said doubtfully, glancing around the dimly lit kitchen as if she expected something unpleasant to leap out of the shadowy corners. "Maybe somewhere else it would be okay. But this place is pretty creepy. Do we really want to be here alone?"

"There are seven of us," Ian pointed out,

"including Trucker. I wouldn't call that being alone."

Cath's eyes moved to Jess. "You're the monitor. What do *you* think?"

Jess was thinking that it might be interesting. It might even be fun. No adult supervision . . . hadn't they all come to college to grow up? She felt terrible about Mrs. Coates's accident, but wouldn't this be the perfect opportunity to take charge of their own lives, with no adult telling them what to do and how to do it?

Before she could answer Cath, Trucker returned from the hospital. "Dislocated hip," he told Jess. "The doctor ordered bed rest. She'll be there for a while. She's okay, though. Worried about you guys. Did you call that friend of hers?"

"Yes. No answer. I'll try again tomorrow." She hesitated. Should they tell Trucker what they'd been discussing? They would need his help. If it turned out that he was the sort of person who felt compelled to call the university and fink on them, they'd simply give up the idea and send for Mrs. Coates's friend Maddie.

But Trucker didn't strike her as the "finking" type.

He wasn't. "Sounds good to me," he said when she'd explained. "But you can go ahead and invite Mrs. Carthew to move in without worrying that she'll accept. I've *met* her. If she agreed at all, it would only be out of a sense of duty. She *hates* everyone under the age of fifty. She'd be miserable here. And so would the rest of us, and that's the truth. Handle it right and she'll turn you down, I promise."

"I *will* call her tomorrow," Jess announced. "That way, we won't be breaking our promise to Mrs. Coates. Maybe we can strike some kind of deal with her where she just pops in occasionally to make sure we're all still breathing and Nightingale Hall is still standing."

Cath looked doubtful, but when everyone else began chattering about ways to make things run more smoothly, she joined in.

Jess ignored her own doubts until everyone stood up, ready to abandon the kitchen for the night. As she left her chair, the wind outside suddenly picked up speed. Leaves and twigs flew at the windows, clawing and scratching at the glass. One of the loose shutters began banging angrily against the brick. The whistle of the wind strengthened, became a wail with a lonely, desolate sound to it. The kitchen light flickered uncertainly.

Cath jumped to her feet. "I don't know about anyone else," she said in a shaky voice, "but that wind shrieking around the house is giving me the creeps!" She hurried out of the room, calling over her shoulder as she left, "If that girl spent nine months in *this* house with that awful wind howling at her, no wonder she committed suicide!"

And then the kitchen light went out, plunging the entire room into darkness.

Chapter 5

Trucker's voice cut through the sudden darkness. "It's okay. It does that sometimes. Loose wire or something, I guess. It's only this kitchen light, though. It won't be dark upstairs. There's a flashlight right here in the drawer." There were fumbling sounds, and then the relief of a flashlight's glow.

Linda and Jess exchanged grateful glances.

Holding the light in front of him, Trucker led the way out of the kitchen and up the stairs.

He was right. The dim glow of the ceiling fixture in the upstairs hall met them as they reached the top of the stairs.

"Okay, you're all set," Trucker said, switching off the flashlight. "I'm going back down and check out that kitchen light. I'm no electrician, but I think I can deal with a loose wire, if that's all it is."

"Please don't electrocute yourself," Jess

begged. She was more convinced than ever that Trucker was handy to have around, especially with Mrs. Coates in the hospital. He knew so much about the house.

He laughed. "Yeah, that would be a *shocking* experience, wouldn't it?"

"Do you live here in the house," she asked, hoping he would say yes. He *had* known where the flashlight was. No one else would have known that.

"I live out back." He tilted his head toward the rear of the house. "Apartment over the garage."

Jess left the three guys in the hall discussing Trucker's apartment and went to her room. Before entering, she watched in envy as Cath and Linda opened the doors to theirs. Hers, she knew, was prettier. Cath's had no flowered wallpaper. Her walls were painted a pale, washed-out blue. And Linda's walls were stark white. Bor-ing.

But . . . no one had *died* in their rooms.

She held her breath as she opened the door. Maybe that awful chill would be gone. Maybe it had never been there in the first place. The excitement of her first day at college could have given her chills . . .

She stepped inside, closing the door behind

her. And sagged against it in disappointment as cold air slapped against her face.

Great room for an Eskimo, she thought. She hurried over to the chest of drawers to yank a sweater from the bottom drawer. As she stood up and slid her arms into the sleeves, she remembered the terrible news Ian had given them and found herself wondering how . . . how the girl Giselle had taken her own life and, her eyes circling the room, where . . . where had she been found? On the bed? On the floor?

Shivering, Jess settled at the desk with pencil and paper. Organizing the household with lists of menus and job assignments would be useful — and would take her mind off Giselle. Tomorrow, she would call Mrs. Coates's friend Madeline. She had promised.

She stayed up later than she should have, reluctant to climb into what had been Giselle's bed.

When her eyelids felt cement-laden and she couldn't stall another minute, she slipped into a long white T-shirt and slid in between the lilac-flowered sheets.

Milo had said the house might be haunted.

Jess pushed her face into the pillow. Milo was so quiet. She'd had better conversations with

toast. Maybe he had tons of morbid thoughts.
Maybe he sat around reading Stephen King and
thinking macabre thoughts about ghosts and
haunted houses and howling wind and foggy
nights.

Maybe he was just kidding.

Or maybe there *was* an uneasy spirit linger-
ing at Nightingale Hall.

Exhausted by the day's excitement, Jess fell
asleep quickly. When she was jolted out of
sleep sometime later, the room was still pitch
black, the house silent. But . . . she had *heard*
something . . . a sound had penetrated her
deep sleep . . . what was it? . . . a scream . . .
someone had screamed . . . loud and shrill and
desperate. . . .

Jess listened carefully.

Nothing.

Tossing her covers aside, she ran to the door
and flung it open. Again, she listened . . .

Still nothing. The house slept on.

But . . . she could still *hear* the scream that
had yanked her so abruptly from sleep. The
terrible sound echoed in her ears.

Maybe . . . could it have been a dream?

Nightmare was more like it.

Listening intently one more time and hearing nothing but the wind stirring the branches of the oak trees outside, Jess closed her door and padded back to the warmth of her bed.

But, with the sound of that desperate scream still ringing in her ears, it was a long time before sleep returned.

The next morning, bright golden rays traced a pathway across the shining hardwood floors in Jess's room. The birds in the ancient oak trees argued furiously over breakfast. The sounds of people slowly awakening filled the second story of Nightingale Hall.

Dressing quickly in denim shorts and a bright green T-shirt, Jess hurried downstairs.

Trucker was in the kitchen, lying on his back under the kitchen sink. "Needs a new elbow," he said cryptically, waving a red-handled wrench at Jess. "Leaking down here."

It struck her that he didn't look much older than the rest of them. "Where did you learn to do all this stuff?" she asked as she poured a cup of coffee. Had he learned to make coffee at the same time he was learning plumbing?

"Around. My old man took off when I was eight. Somebody had to take care of things. I was elected."

His father had taken a hike? Jess made no

comment. Her parents' divorce had been painful. But at least she sometimes saw her father. Her parents were still friendly.

Footsteps pounded down the stairs and Ian, Jon, and Milo burst into the kitchen, proclaiming starvation. Linda and Cath followed a few minutes later.

"Anyone hear anything . . . weird last night?" Jess asked when they were all in the kitchen.

"Just that stupid wind," Cath said crankily.

Linda shook her head no, Milo shrugged, and Jon said with a grin, "I was too busy having a great dream about Kim Basinger."

"Why?" Ian asked Jess. "Did *you* hear something?"

Learning that no one else had heard the scream convinced Jess that she had been dreaming. Probably the result of Ian's porch horror story.

"I guess not," she told him, handing him the coffee pot. "Must have been the wind, like Cath said."

Breakfast was a haphazard affair. Linda, scheduled for her first swim practice, ate as if she hadn't eaten in days. Cath ate nothing, sipping quietly on a cup of black coffee, while Jon yearned loudly for bacon and eggs and bagels as he crunched cold cereal. Milo, his head down, drew intricate designs on his toast with a jelly knife. Jess and Ian talked about school. Too excited to eat much, she drank juice and wrote her name in all three of the notebooks she'd brought with her.

By the time they left for campus, Mrs. Coates's immaculate kitchen looked as if it had been picked up by a maniacal giant and dropped upside down, spilling the contents out of cupboards, drawers, and pantry.

Trucker surveyed the damage, shrugged, and went back to work.

On campus, nervous, excited freshmen, trying hard to look cool and confident, milled around outside the beautiful ivy-covered brick buildings. Upperclassmen smiled condescendingly as they walked by.

The first girl Jess met at registration inside Butler Hall asked her which dorm she lived in. "I'm at Miller, myself," the tall, thin, brown-haired girl said. "I think it's the best. So, where are you? Briggs? Devereaux? The Quad?"

"I'm not on campus," Jess admitted. The hall was very crowded, and she didn't see Ian anywhere. In the crowd, she'd been separated from her housemates. Maybe they were in another building. "I'm up on the hill, at Nightingale Hall."

"Off-campus? Oh." The girl looked disappointed. Then a glimmer of curiosity slid across her face. "Nightingale Hall? You mean that creepy place with all those big trees?"

Jess nodded. She wished the line for registration would move faster. It was stuffy in the hall. Everyone else seemed to be with people they knew.

"I heard something about that place," the brown-haired girl said. Her pale eyes searched Jess's face. "Something weird."

Jess feigned innocence. "Really?" She did *not* feel like discussing that story about Giselle.

"Yeah. Like, no one wants to stay there." She paused for dramatic effect. Her lips curved in a smile that hinted at meanness. "That's why they had to get freshmen to stay there, because they don't know any better. Because . . ." the pale eyes glinted, "because some girl *died* there!"

When Jess said nothing, the girl added, "But you probably didn't know about that, did you?"

"Of course I knew," Jess said lightly. "It doesn't bother me, or anyone else at the house." She spotted Ian's long, dark hair and white T-shirt. "Excuse me, I see my friends over there. 'Bye!" Then, even though the line Ian, Jon, and

Cath were in was longer than hers, she dashed over to join them.

"Whew!" she told Ian, "am I ever glad to see you! I got tangled up with The Great Inquisitor over there."

Ian nodded. "Yeah, I know what you mean. I've told three people I'm staying at Nightingale Hall. They all looked at me like I had a screw loose. I think it's because nothing was ever resolved about that girl who died."

Jess looked up at him. "Come again?"

"Well, the official verdict was apparent suicide. The key word there being *apparent*. Meaning they couldn't prove it for sure. Trucker said there wasn't much of an investigation. The school wanted it hushed up, I guess. Understandable if you think about it. "But," Ian glanced around the crowded hall, "judging by the way people react to Nightingale Hall, I'd say the word definitely got out."

Cath had been listening. Her thin, oval face seemed tightly pinched. "It sounds so gross," she said in a near-whisper. "Someone told me she was found hanging from the light fixture. Mrs. Coates found her." Cath shuddered. "It must have been awful for her."

The light fixture? Jess thought, repulsed. In *my* room?

Then the line moved forward, Jon mentioned a party the following night, and the conversation about the death in Jess's room ended.

But she couldn't help wondering exactly what "*apparent* suicide" meant. Didn't "apparent" mean there was a question about Giselle's death?

What, exactly, *was* the question?

Chapter 6

Throughout the day, Jess was too busy registering for classes and, later, buying incredibly expensive secondhand textbooks at the campus bookstore to dwell on unanswered questions about a girl she'd never even met.

"I can't believe my book bill!" she complained as the group gathered outside the bookstore. "I could have bought a new car with that money. Or taken a trip around the world."

"Freshmen aren't allowed to have cars on campus," Jon pointed out, clearly annoyed by the fact. "If we were, I would have breezed past you yesterday, tooling up the driveway in my red BMW."

Of course his car would be red. And Jess bet it was a convertible, too.

"My red BMW convertible," Jon added dreamily. "But," he added brightly, "since I'm not living on campus, I can have a car. I checked. My dad's bringing it up this weekend. We'll have wheels!"

No one responded. They were all sure that if Jon had wheels, he'd be using those wheels for dates, not transporting his housemates around town. He looked disappointed at their lack of reaction to his news.

"Listen," Milo said as they began walking, "if we'd pooled the money we spent on books, we could have bought our own *dorm*! Then we could kiss Nightingale Hall good-bye. People have been giving me flack about it all day."

"Me, too," Cath said. "I'm not telling anyone where I live from now on. I'll say I'm camping out behind the gym or something."

"Right," Jon agreed, smiling at Cath. "Maybe I'll say I live in my car."

Jess began leafing through her German book. "Well," she said ruefully, "I bought used books, but they weren't that much cheaper." Closing the book and thrusting it into her backpack, she added, "I just wish someone had warned me about how expensive college was going to be. I would have saved more money instead of throwing it away on trivial things, like food and clothing."

Ian helped her adjust the backpack. "Look at it this way. You've registered for classes and bought your books. You are now an official college student." He grinned down at her. "So? You feel any different than you did in high school?"

"Yeah, I feel a lot poorer!" But as they began walking across campus toward the highway, she realized that she did feel different. Older? No, not really. Maybe . . . more . . . free? A little more independent? Out on her own, away from family, responsible, now, for herself. Scary thought, that "responsible" part. But, exciting, too.

"I got every class I wanted," Linda said happily. "Pretty easy schedule, too, with plenty of time for swim practice and meets."

"My schedule isn't too bad, either," Jon said. "After all, my major is parties, sports, and . . . *women*." He grinned at Cath, who looked away, embarrassed.

The trek from school to Nightingale Hall on such a beautiful day took only about ten minutes. Cars full of students passed them, on their way to the long, silver diner called Burgers Etc., a popular place for gathering after classes. Halfway between the campus and town, on the highway, it provided quick and easy access to good food, good music, and fun.

But the residents of Nightingale Hall wanted to get home and drop off their books before deciding how to spend the rest of the day. And Jess was planning to call Mrs. Coates's friend, hoping to convince her that they could manage on their own. So far, they were doing okay, although the kitchen was still a disaster from breakfast.

She was relieved to learn that Madeline Carthew wasn't any more eager to join them at Nightingale Hall than they were to have her. Her tone of voice upon receiving the invitation indicated she would rather undergo oral surgery.

"Of course I'd *love* to help," she said nervously when she'd told Jess she'd been expecting her call. "Isobel is my dear friend, and I know my duty when I see it. But oh my, all that rock music and young people running in and out of the house would be so bad for my nerves. I'm not all that well myself, you know. And," she added hastily, "it isn't as if you need a babysitter. My goodness, you're all high school graduates, practically adults."

Practically? Jess grinned. It sounded like they weren't going to have a live-in babysitter, after all.

"But I do take my duty to my friends seriously . . ."

Darn!

". . . so I promised Isobel I would look in on all of you from time to time. And you must promise me that you will call me the very second you need anything." Pause. "Anything at *all*, dear."

Jess was still grinning when she hung up.

That taken care of, she went to her room and emptied her backpack onto the bed.

Picking up her new books one at a time, she began leafing through them, enjoying the feel of the soft, dog-eared pages, the "used" smell of them, trying to imagine a face behind every name written on each frontispiece. Someone named Susan Braun had owned her math book. What would a Susan Braun look like? Tall and thin? Intelligent face, with wire-rimmed glasses? Pretty, with a nice smile? Someone who actually understood the intricate-looking equations in the middle of the book?

There were two names in her history book. Craig J. Winters, III, which sounded to Jess like tons and tons of money, probably all handed down by Craig J. Winters the first and second. And Tom Wilson, a nice, simple, ordinary name that told her nothing except that she probably would like someone who wrote his name "Tom" instead of the more formal "Thomas."

She opened her English Lit book.

And sucked in her breath as she read the name.

Written in a delicate, precise longhand, on the right-hand corner at the top of the page, was the name, *Giselle McKendrick*.

And underneath that, in case Jess should have any doubts about which Giselle this might be, were the words, *Nightingale Hall*.

Chapter 7

Jess sat in silence for several minutes, her fingers gingerly tracing the letters that spelled Giselle McKendrick's name.

Then, giving herself a stern shake, she murmured, "I'm being ridiculous. Of *course* Giselle bought books at this college. She was a *student* here."

But . . . wasn't it incredibly weird that she, Jess, out of hundreds of freshmen, had bought the English Lit book previously owned by the only girl at Salem University who had . . . died . . . the preceding spring?

Not to mention the fact that she was living in the same girl's lilac-flowered bedroom and sleeping in her lilac-sheeted bed?

"I could trade this book in," she told the empty room. "All freshmen use this book. Someone who hasn't heard the rumors about Nightingale Hall or doesn't recognize Giselle's name would trade with me." She slapped the book's cover shut.

"I could avoid that page," she said aloud. But she knew that wasn't the answer. Giselle's name might be written only on that one page, but Giselle's eyes had focused on many pages, her fingers had tap-tapped on others while she tried to concentrate, and the book itself had probably nestled cozily inside Giselle's backpack during her trips to and from campus.

"I can't deal with this," she said to herself. "First thing Monday morning, I find someone who's never heard of Nightingale Hall or Giselle McKendrick and I dump this book!"

With that decision made, she put the books aside and went downstairs to the bright and sunny kitchen.

She made some order out of the chaos and put soup on the stove to heat.

Dinner, which everyone helped pull together, was fun. The excitement of the day kept everyone from complaining about the blackened hot dogs and lukewarm vegetable soup. No one cared. Even Jon ate without complaint.

But when Cath began talking about the classes she'd registered for and all the work she already had to do, Jon cried, "Puh-leeze! Can we not talk about classes and assignments and depressing stuff like that? I'll lose my appetite." He said this as he reached for his fourth hot dog.

"Who's up for exploring the local hangouts?" Jess asked.

Almost everyone enthusiastically agreed with her suggestion.

Only Milo dissented. "Count me out," he said crankily. "Waste of time. I'd rather go night-fishing. Haven't tried the creek yet." He stood up, running a hand through his unruly beige hair. "Everyone and his brother will be out running around town tonight. I hate crowds. Besides, I'd rather commune with nature."

It was obvious he'd made up his mind. They let him go with no further argument.

The disappointment on Linda's round, pink face was quickly replaced by a dreamy look of admiration.

She's seeing the soul of a poet in Milo, Jess thought, her amusement mixed with concern for Linda. He didn't seem at all interested, and she didn't seem very thick-skinned.

Their attempts at cleanup were halfhearted. They were all anxious to begin exploring the town. Grateful for paper plates and cups and feeling only a little guilty about cluttering up some distant landfill, Jess ran upstairs to change her clothes.

She dressed in jeans and the gray Salem sweatshirt she had purchased that day at the bookstore. Her guilt over the added expense of the shirt was not as easily dismissed as her ecological guilt over the paper plates. She knew she shouldn't have spent the money.

But everyone else had bought one, except, of course, Milo. And something had come over her there in the crowded bookstore. With the load of college textbooks in her arms, she had been seized suddenly by a fierce, overwhelming need to claim the bookstore, the university, the classmates surrounding her, as her *own*. Her *place*. Her new life. And it seemed to her that wearing the soft, thick gray sweatshirt with the Salem University seal on the front would help her do that.

Satisfied that the sweatshirt fit exactly right — not too skimpy, not too baggy — she ran lightly down the stairs, determined to have fun on this, her first night as a duly registered college student.

And they *did* have fun. Even quiet, intense Cath, looking exceptionally pretty in a lacy white blouse and jeans, laughed at Jon's corny jokes and cracked a few of her own.

Pennsylvania Avenue teemed with college students. They spilled out of restaurants, diners, and shops. The avenue running parallel to the peaceful river became a bumper-to-bumper ribbon of honking cars crammed with shouting, laughing passengers, their radios set at full volume.

"Good thing we walked," Jon said as the group ambled along the crowded avenue. "Much as I miss my Beemer, there's no way I'd sandwich it into that traffic."

Jess liked the idea that a fifteen-minute walk in one direction brought them straight into town, while a ten-minute walk in the opposite direction took them straight to campus. Nightingale Hall might not be a castle, but it was well-located.

Cath groaned at the crowd, but Jess was excited, eager to join in. They decided to try a place called Duffy's first. It was overflowing with students, and looked like fun. Inside, loud music played and students stood around in clusters, listening to the music and checking each other out. Some were playing pool or video games.

When Jess spotted Trucker ambling through the throng alone, his usual coveralls replaced by jeans and a deep blue T-shirt, she invited him to join their group. "You know your way around town better than we do," she said, ignoring Cath's expression of distaste.

"But he's the *handyman!*" Cath whispered as a smiling Trucker joined them. "He isn't even a *student!*"

"Yeah, I am," he said amiably, overhearing her. He seemed unruffled by her remarks. His blue eyes, Jess noticed, had tiny flecks of green in them, the color of seawater. "Two night courses. Registered this morning." He grinned. "I figure, at this pace, I'll be crippled with arthritis by the time I get my degree. But it's better than not going at all."

"Good for you," Ian applauded, and Jess nodded agreement.

Then Ian spotted a photo booth in one corner, and he urged Jess inside.

"Oh, I hate these things, Ian!" she protested, pulling back. "The pictures always look like I should have a prison number scrawled across the bottom."

But he refused to let go of her hand. "C'mon, Jess, we need a record of what we looked like on our first day at college."

"Go on, Jess," Linda urged with an impish

grin. "Jon and Cath and I will go next." She flushed, remembering Trucker and added lamely, "And Trucker."

"Not me," he said, moving aside. "I'd break the camera."

No, he wouldn't, Jess thought. Without that stupid baseball cap he always wears, he's really good-looking.

The thought surprised her.

"C'mon," Ian said. He pulled Jess inside the booth and closed the black curtain around them.

When he was seated, she sat on his lap, since there was nowhere else to sit. Although Ian sat perfectly still for his picture and smiled into the camera, Jess stuck out her tongue, crossed her eyes, and covered her face with her hands, peering out devilishly from between her splayed fingers. When Ian yelled at her to cut it out, she said, "Oh, what's the difference? They're going to be terrible, anyway."

But they weren't. Outside the booth, Jess grabbed the thin strip of photos from Ian's hands. "Let me see!" Jon and Cath and Linda clustered around her. "I guarantee you," she said jokingly as she held up the strip to inspect it, "I will look so awful . . ."

Then her voice trailed off and a puzzled silence fell over the group as they all looked down at the picture in Jess's hand. Trucker moved forward to see why they weren't exploding in laughter.

"I don't get it," Jess said slowly, peering more closely at the film strip. "Ian?"

They all stared silently at the pictures in Jess's hand. They stared at Ian, smiling, and at Jess, her tongue out in one picture, her eyes crossed in another, her face hidden behind her hands in the bottom two shots.

And they stared at the clouded but visible image of a girl with long, pale hair and a painfully sad expression on a very pretty face, looking solemnly into the camera from behind Ian and Jess.

Only two people had gone into the photo booth.

But there were three people in the pictures.

Chapter 8

"Who *is* that?" Linda was the first to ask. Jon followed up with, "I didn't see anyone else go into that booth with you."

"No one *did*." Jess's eyes met Ian's. "Right? It was just us, you and me."

Ian shrugged. "Double exposure. Ruined our pictures! Want to try it again?"

"Double exposure?" Doubt sounded in Jess's voice. "In a booth?"

"Sure. Someone . . . this girl . . ." Ian tapped the filmstrip, "went in ahead of us. Paid her dollar, got her pictures, and left. But the film must not have advanced automatically. So it took our pictures right on top of hers. That's why her image is kind of cloudy." Ian turned to Jon. "You guys better not try it. The film's probably still stuck. Don't waste your money."

Since one of Ian's hobbies was photography

and Jess had never owned a camera, she would have felt silly arguing with him about the pictures. He seemed so positive. And what other explanation could there be?

Taking her hand in his, the pictures forgotten, Ian led her toward the room with the pool tables.

But Jess couldn't dismiss the odd occurrence so quickly. That girl . . . the fuzzy image hovering in their pictures . . . she looked so sad. Freshman blues? First time away from home, hadn't made any friends yet . . . was that all the sadness in her eyes meant? Probably.

Still . . . would someone who felt like that go to an arcade? Alone? And have pictures taken, also alone, in a photo booth?

I don't *think* so, Jess told herself. That wasn't the kind of thing you did when you were miserable. What you did then was go home and hide in bed with the covers over your head.

Her companions, laughing hilariously at one of Jon's jokes, had already forgotten the pictures.

Jess tried to do the same. But several times during the rest of the evening, Jess found herself searching the crowd for any sign of a pretty girl with long, pale hair and a sad face.

Telling herself she was in danger of spoiling a perfectly good time, she forced the skinny strip of photos out of her mind.

Later, on the way home in the bed of Trucker's brown pick-up truck, she listened absent-mindedly as Jon cheerfully described how he'd once been dumped by the prettiest girl in school.

"She sent me a tape of that song about so many ways to leave your lover. Remember that one?"

Nods all around. The balmy early September warmth wrapped its arms around them, ruffled their hair.

"Well, she sent a note along with the tape," Jon continued. "All it said was, 'Get the idea?'" He nodded in chagrin. "I got it, all right. I don't have to be hit over the head with an AK-47."

"Weren't you mad?" Linda wanted to know. "Sounds kind of mean to me. If somebody dumped *me* like that, I'd be furious."

Jon shook his head. "Nah. I thought it was kind of clever. Very creative girl," he added, admiration in his voice. "And drop-dead gorgeous. Blonde hair, robin's egg blue eyes . . ."

Jess thought she heard regret in the words. Maybe Jon was only joking to hide his hurt.

She was suddenly ashamed of how quickly she'd judged him. Here he was, poking fun at himself, letting everyone know he'd been dumped. Not many guys would do that. And at the same time, he seemed to be admitting that he'd once had strong feelings for someone. Maybe he wasn't as shallow as she'd thought.

Contrite, Jess beamed a sincerely friendly smile in Jon's direction.

But he was concentrating all of his attention on Cath, who, now that the evening of fun was almost over, had reverted back to her quiet reserve.

They would make a gorgeous couple, Jess thought. If Cath ever let Jon get close enough.

When they arrived at Nightingale Hall, Jess joined the others foraging for food in the night-darkened and now chilly kitchen. The windows behind the sink, sun filled during the day, reflected at night only an eerie, empty blackness. No golden rays warmed the tired linoleum flooring and the small round wooden table and chairs and the stark-white appliances.

Jess shivered. As she walked past the cellar door, it flew open, sending out a mass of cold air from the gloomy underbelly of the house. Jess, gasping in surprise, was reminded of the wave of frigid air that greeted her whenever she entered her room. Maybe she'd been right about its source. This air felt the same.

Closing the door and latching it, she joined the hungry group analyzing the refrigerator's contents. Trucker handed her a carton of ice cream. Glancing toward the cellar door, he said, "I keep forgetting to replace that latch. Door swings open all the time."

"It's cold down there." She remembered what she'd meant to ask him. "Could that air be leaking into my room, maybe from the chimney? It's colder in the room than it is out in the hall."

"Maybe. I'll check it out."

"Thanks, Trucker.'

She wrinkled her nose in distaste. "The air from the cellar smells moldy." She grinned. "There aren't any bodies buried down there, are there?" Then, remembering Giselle, she flushed with sudden shame.

Trucker seemed unperturbed. "Not as far as I know. Just in case, you can keep the door up here latched. When I work down there, I'll use the outside cellar doors."

She knew the doors he referred to. They were old-fashioned wooden panels slanted into the ground above stone steps leading down into the cellar. Her Wisconsin grandparents had the same arrangement.

But their cellar smelled better.

By the time they'd all eaten and thoroughly dissected their first day at college, fatigue had settled in and they were all ready to call it a day.

Jess hesitated only for a second or two in the doorway to her room. Was she going to need flannel pajamas to sleep?

She was. The room hadn't warmed up at all.

Get used to it, she told herself. It's no big deal.

Exhausted, she slept like a long-distance runner after a big race.

The following week passed in a blur of new faces, new classes, new routines. The work, Jess found, was harder than in high school, but a lot more interesting. So many books to read, so many papers to write, all involving hours of research. German assignments to translate, math exercises to labor over. The math, she decided, was designed to weed out the weak from the strong. "If you can actually do this stuff," she told Ian as they studied in the first-floor library at Nightingale Hall, "they let you stay in school and get a degree, which, if you *can* do this stuff, you probably don't even *need*."

Cath nodded. "And if you *can't* do it," she grumbled, her head bent over a book, "they send you home, and your parents disown you and kick you out of the house to wander through town the rest of your life carrying all of your belongings in a shopping bag."

Everyone laughed. But Jess suspected Cath had just told them her worst nightmare.

In spite of the heavy work load, which Cath agonized over, driving them all crazy, and Milo pretty much ignored, they all found time for other things. Jon, whose beloved red car had been delivered, went out almost every night with a different girl, although his eyes said he was still waiting for Cath to acknowledge his existence. Linda was busy with swim practices and meets. Ian spent hours taking photographs for *The Chronicle*, the campus newspaper, and occasionally joined Milo and Trucker at the creek behind the house for some fishing.

The following weekend, there were parties, a concert, a football game. Jess and the others enjoyed themselves, but Cath shut herself in her room, studying. Her face lost what little color it had had and her lips became pinched and tight with stress. Her dark eyes took on the look of a trapped rabbit.

Jess couldn't think of any way to help.

Every night, after a haphazard meal of soup and sandwiches, or hamburgers and french fries, or spaghetti, and the desserts Madeline Carthew dropped off to assuage her conscience, Cath hurried off to her room, her ballet-slippered feet slap-slapping up the stairs with urgency.

"Doesn't she ever relax?" Jon muttered, annoyed. "All work and no play makes life pretty grim."

"And all play and no *work*," Jess said pointedly, "makes a college dropout."

Jon grinned. "Yeah, yeah. I'll get to it. I'm just getting acclimated, that's all."

On Sunday evening, Cath gobbled half a bacon, lettuce, and tomato sandwich, dumped her plate in the sink, which was still filled with encrusted cereal bowls from breakfast, and announced that she had a "crucial" lit paper to work on.

"It's due tomorrow and I'm not done with my bibliography." She aimed a sharp glance at Milo. "But at least I've started. Have you even done your outline yet, Milo?"

"Brilliant minds," Milo said, tilting his chair back against the kitchen counter, "do not employ methods as pedestrian as outlining."

Cath hooted in derision.

"And while *you* slave away up in your dark little cave," Milo added, "I'll be outside gratefully gulping in some much-needed fresh air."

"It's raining, Milo."

"So? A little rain never killed anyone, and the fishing is great when it's raining." Milo freed his fishing pole from its customary position between the stove and refrigerator and left the house.

Disgusted, Cath hurried upstairs to her room.

"She does work too hard," Jess commented to Ian as they loaded the dishwasher. Linda had gone off to a swim meet, Jon to a party, and Trucker, who had begun eating dinner with them at Jess's invitation, had gone to join Milo at the creek. "She looks so tired all the time, and she's wound tighter than a spring."

Ian agreed. "If she doesn't learn to let off some of that steam, she'll explode. College isn't like high school. Some people can't handle the difference."

Several hours later, as Jess was finishing her German translation and thinking that Ian's eyes were the warmest brown she'd ever seen, his dire prediction rang in her ears. A door slammed open, footsteps ran down the hall and stopped at Jess's door. Cath's voice, edged in hysteria, shouted, "Jess! Open the door, open it! Let me in!"

Chapter 9

"Jessica, let me *in*!" Panic etched Cath's words.

Remembering Ian's prediction about Cath, Jess ran to the door and threw it open.

Cath's narrow face was ash-gray. Her dark eyes echoed the panic in her voice. "What am I going to *do*?" she cried. "The paper I worked so hard on is *gone*! I was sitting on my bed working on my bibliography, and when I finished it I went to the desk for my paper. That's where I put it. But it's not there. It's gone, Jess!"

Jess went weak with relief. "Oh, Cath, I thought someone was trying to *kill* you! You're hysterical over a missing *paper*?"

"What's going on?" Linda called as she hurried to Jess's room. Her hair was still wet from swimming and she was wrapped in a white terrycloth robe.

Ian followed her, while Milo lingered in his own doorway. Three different kinds of music wafted from the open rooms and mixed together in a discordant blend of rock, classical, and East Indian melodies.

"That missing paper is important," Cath retorted. "It's due tomorrow morning. And my average in lit class isn't that high."

Meaning, Jess thought, a B+ instead of an A.

But Cath's hands were trembling, her eyes glittering with threatening tears. "If I don't turn in that paper, I'll be lucky to pull a C in there! A *C*!"

Jess couldn't imagine falling apart over a simple C. She'd had her share of them and the earth hadn't stopped spinning on its axis.

"Maybe you moved your paper," she told Cath reassuringly. "C'mon, we'll all help you look for it."

They looked everywhere: on Cath's desk, in her dresser drawers, under the bed, in the closet, in the pockets of her jeans and raincoat . . . but there was no sign of the missing paper.

When they were ready to admit defeat, Jess and Ian sat on Cath's bed. She stood in the center of the room, wringing her hands. "How can I show up in class tomorrow without that paper?"

"Cath," Jess said, "can't you tell your professor the truth? You can't be the first student to lose a paper, can you? Maybe he'll give you more time."

Cath turned on her. "But I don't *lose* things, Jess! Ever." After a moment, she added, "Someone *took* my paper."

There was a shocked silence.

Cath's face was a narrow mask of white. "And *that* means," she said, her voice tremulous, "that someone was in my *room*. Someone went through my *things*!"

They could all see that the thought horrified her.

"Took your paper?" Ian said. "You mean, as in *stole* it?"

Cath nodded.

"Honestly, Cath," Linda said, "why on earth would anyone *steal* your paper?"

Cath, her lips firmly pressed together, looked at Milo. "You have the same paper due tomorrow," she said, "and you haven't even done your *outline*."

All eyes moved to Milo, leaning against Cath's desk.

His eyes behind the wire-rimmed glasses narrowed. "I'm not hearing an accusation here, am I?"

"My paper was right here on the desk, beside the lamp. And now it isn't. Did you finish *your* paper?"

Milo stood up very straight. His face flushed with anger. "No, I didn't. Don't worry about it."

"The question is," Cath said, her head high, her dark eyes very bright, "why aren't *you* worried about it?" Suddenly, she turned and ran out of the room, heading straight for Milo's room across the hall.

"Hey!" he cried, running after her, "what do you think you're doing?"

What she was doing, they all discovered as they followed and gathered in the doorway to Milo's room, was racing around like a crazy person, tossing papers and clothing and CDs in the air, her dark hair flying about her face, her eyes wild.

"It's here," she babbled as she tossed a pile of books on the floor. "I *know* my paper is here. You took it so you wouldn't have to write a paper of your own."

Linda gasped. "Milo would never do that," she cried.

"You're crazy!" Milo shouted, scooping up the discarded books. "You've really lost it, you know? I never touched your stupid paper. I never went near your room." He lunged at Cath as she dumped a handful of CDs on the hardwood floor. "Cath, cut it *out!*" Bending to pick up the disks, he appealed to the others, still in the doorway, their mouths open. "Stop her, will you? She's wrecking my room."

And even though it seemed to Jess that the room had already been a wreck before Cath arrived, she stepped forward to grasp Cath's wrist, saying softly, "Okay, that's enough. He says the paper isn't here."

"Could have blown out your window," Ian suggested. "While we were eating. Was your window open?"

Drained, exhausted, Cath sagged against Jess. "I . . . I don't know. I don't remember."

"Well," Linda said, moving into the room to stoop and pick up some papers and a maroon jacket Cath had tossed on the floor, "I personally think you've got a lot of nerve, Cath. Accusing Milo of *stealing!*" She smiled at Milo and reached out to touch his hand. "We all know he wouldn't do anything like that."

Actually, Jess thought, we don't know any such thing. Everyone *seems* nice enough here

78

at Nightingale Hall, but we don't *really* know each other. Not yet. Aloud, she said, "C'mon, Cath, let's go back to your room and figure out what to do."

"What's to figure?" Cath said bitterly. "I don't have any choice. I'll be up all night rewriting that paper, that's all. But," leveling a look of fury at Milo and Linda, who stood beside him, "don't think I'll forget about this, because I won't!" Then, in a low voice directed only at Milo, she added, "Get *this*! You probably thought I wouldn't have time to redo the paper, but I'll finish it if it kills me. So forget about turning in the one you stole, unless you want to be kicked out of this school for cheating."

She ran from the room. The door to her own room slammed so hard the posters on Milo's walls flapped wildly.

Jess decided it might be a good idea to let Cath work on her anger alone. But as Ian walked her back down the hallway to her own room, she said quietly, "That paper couldn't have just walked away. And Cath doesn't seem like the sort of person who misplaces things."

"That's for sure."

"Do *you* think Milo took it?" she asked Ian.

"Why would he? Cath's right, he can't turn it in."

"I know, but he could have underestimated Cath. Thinking that she wouldn't have time to finish a rewrite." Jess leaned against the wall outside her room. Sighing, she said, "There's something about this place. I wish I could figure out what it is. I know it's getting to Cath. I don't think it's just the pressure of classes that's turning her into a maniac."

Ian ran a gentle finger along the frown lines in Jess's forehead, smoothing them out. "What you need," he said, "is food. Let's roust everyone out of their rooms and raid the refrigerator."

"Ian, I'm kind of tired . . ."

"That means your engine needs fuel. C'mon, I saw microwave popcorn in the kitchen. Lots of it. It's calling to me." He tilted his head. "Ian, I-an!" He began running up and down the hallway, pounding on doors, calling, "Popcorn break, everyone! Move those tired old bodies down to the kitchen, pronto!"

Laughing helplessly, Jess said, "You sound like a cheerleader. Or a drill sergeant." But she felt better already.

Cath's door didn't open. Jess hadn't expected it to.

Everyone else seemed grateful for a study break. They all pounded downstairs to the kitchen. Milo had apparently recovered from Cath's accusation . Ian made popcorn and Linda filled glasses with soda. They ate and drank and talked about their classes and an upcoming formal, the Fall Ball, which Linda had heard was "a very big deal." Jon arrived from campus just in time to share the last bag of popcorn.

Feeling relaxed and comfortable in spite of Cath's absence, Jess smiled at Ian and said, "This was a great idea."

He looked pleased. "Stick with me, baby," he said in a mock Humphrey Bogart voice, "and the sky's the limit. Anything you want, name it."

"I'd settle for a warmer kitchen," she said, leaning over to nestle into Ian's red-sweatered bulk. "Can you manage that for me?"

"Just come in June," Linda said, licking salt from her fingers. "This place is an oven then."

"In June?" Jess said. "How do you know?"

Linda got up to take her glass to the sink. "I was here for that orientation day they had. Weren't you?"

"No." She *had* wanted to see the university before she made up her mind, but she hadn't had time. The brochures they'd sent had had to suffice.

"Ian was here," Linda said, turning away

from the sink. "And Jon. I saw them on campus."

Ian nodded. "Came with a bunch of guys from my high school. They didn't like it, but I did."

Jess felt a little left out. They'd all visited campus last June?

"It was a scorcher that day," Linda said. "It almost made me think about finding a school in Alaska. But everyone kept saying it was just a weird heat wave, not normal, so I decided to come here, anyway. But I didn't know then that I'd be living at Nightingale Hall. It's probably a good thing that I didn't see it first. I might have changed my mind and gone somewhere else."

Jess could understand that. If she had known she was going to be sleeping in the room of a girl who had died, would she have moved in, anyway?

I don't *think* so, she told herself.

"So," Ian said, standing up, "anyone sorry they decided to come here?" Smiling, his eyes found Jess's. "I know I'm not. Look at the great class of people this university attracts."

"Speaking of people," Jon said, "where's Cath? How come she's not pigging out like the rest of us?"

Milo jumped to his feet and left the room. Linda quickly followed.

It was left to Ian and Jess to fill Jon in on the trouble between the three.

He took Cath's side, which didn't surprise Jess. "Milo's too far off center," he said as they left the kitchen.

"I think he's just shy," Jess said.

But hadn't she, at first, thought Milo was unfriendly, and a bit odd? And that look on his face when Cath accused him of stealing . . . that hadn't looked like simple anger. There'd been something strange in that look.

Something that scared Jess.

Chapter 10

Bright sunshine lighting up Jess's room the following morning failed to dispel the pervasive chill. Goose bumps formed on her arms as she dressed quickly in jeans and a white T-shirt that read, *I IS A COLLEGE FRESHMAN*, a going-away present from her sister Nell. She ran a brush through the shiny dark hair that was beginning to grow longer. The short haircut had been easy to take care of, but not much fun. Now a few thick strands curled softly around her high cheekbones.

Maybe, she thought, I'll actually be able to do something interesting with it by the time the Fall Ball rolls around. Laughing softly at her own unintentional pun, Jess escaped into the warmth of the hall.

In the kitchen, Linda was expressing disgust over Jon's choice of breakfast.

"A hot dog and ice cream?" She made a gagging gesture. "Your body is a temple, Jon, and you're tossing a wrecking ball at it."

Jon continued munching with pleasure. "Food is food," he mumbled around a mouthful of hot dog bun. Swallowing, he added, "You see anything wrong with this body?"

As Jess moved to the refrigerator for a glass of juice, she thought about the formal Linda had mentioned the night before. Hurry up and ask me to that dance, she ordered Ian silently. Time's a-wastin'. A boy in her history class had been hanging around a lot lately. What if he asked her first? Would it be totally rotten to turn him down, hoping that Ian would ask her? And then what if Ian didn't?

"What did Maddie bring us yesterday?" Linda asked, lifting a blue cloth napkin to peer into the wicker picnic hamper sitting on the kitchen counter. "Gee, isn't it great that she gets rid of her guilt about not moving in with us by baking goodies?"

"What would I do without her?" Jon said gratefully, biting into a strawberry muffin from Maddie's most recent care package.

Laughing, Jess wondered where Cath was. Had she already left for school? Had she finished the essay rewrite?

As if on cue, Cath appeared in the kitchen

doorway. She looked terrible. Her eyes were shadowed with purplish raccoon-rings, her hair a tangle of dark waves hanging limply around her pale, strained face. She was wearing the same tan skirt and green blouse she'd worn the day before. The skirt was wrinkled, the blouse drooping over the waistband.

It's not just her clothes that looked wrinkled, Jess thought with a wave of compassion. Every inch of her looks wrinkled, as if she'd spent the night tumbling around in a clothes dryer.

Cath waved a sheaf of white paper in the air. To Milo, she said, "I finished, just like I said I would. So you can forget about turning in that paper you stole from me." Her smile was cold. "You wouldn't want to be accused of cheating, would you? Although for someone like you, that probably wouldn't be a first." Aiming one last contemptuous glance in Milo's direction, she hurried from the room.

The front door slammed a moment later.

Shaking his head in disgust, Milo got up, muttered, "That girl is crazy! I never went near her room," and left the kitchen. Linda did the same. Their footsteps echoed through the house as they went upstairs.

Jon followed a moment later.

"Cath is so positive that Milo took her paper,"

Jess said to Ian when they were alone. "She's never going to forgive him. We'll have to draw up battle lines to keep them away from each other."

Ian nodded. "What's the quote? The one that goes, 'United we stand, divided we fall'? Sounds like us, doesn't it?"

Jess agreed. We *are* living in a house divided, she thought dispiritedly. "I wonder if Milo ever *did* do his paper?"

Ian, at the back door with an overflowing wastebasket in hand, asked, "You think he took Cath's paper, don't you?"

She was saved from a reply by the peal of the front doorbell. Ian went out back with the trash and Jess ran into the hall to yank open the front door.

A short, stocky young man in a military uniform stood before her, twirling his Army cap in his hands. His straw-colored hair was cut very short and neatly parted to one side. He had deep brown eyes that seemed sad to Jess, almost melancholy.

But he smiled at her. "I'm Avery McKendrick," he said. "I had a telephone conversation with Mrs. Coates a few weeks ago about picking up my sister's trunk. She said it would be okay."

"McKendrick?" Jess echoed. McKendrick? As in . . . ?

"Giselle was my sister," he said quietly.

"Oh, I'm . . . I'm sorry," Jess stammered, "please come in."

He stepped inside. "Thanks. I'd have been here sooner, but I was stationed in the Philippines. I just came back to the States last week. Is Mrs. Coates in?"

"No. No, she's . . . she isn't." Jess searched for the right words. "You . . . you said you came for your sister's trunk?"

Avery McKendrick nodded. "It's in the cellar. There was a guy in overalls outside . . . dark hair? He volunteered to go find the trunk for me. I'm not sure we can manage it alone, though." He smiled sadly. "My sister was a pack rat. She saved everything. The trunk probably weighs a ton."

Jess would have gone in search of Ian to help with the trunk, but Milo, Jon, and Linda, books in hand, came hurrying down the stairs.

"Well, hey, Milo!" Avery said, extending a hand, "how *are* you? Never expected to find *you* here. So you decided to go to school, after all? That's great!"

Jess stared as Milo, looking uncomfortable,

shook Avery's hand. "You two know each other?" she asked.

"Who *is* he?" Linda asked Jess in a near-whisper.

"He's Giselle McKendrick's brother," Jess said clearly, adding, "Milo, I didn't know you knew Giselle."

"Really?" Linda breathed, giving Milo an inquiring look.

"Well, sure," Giselle's brother said. "Milo practically lived at our house when he was a kid. He went all through school with my sister. They walked home together every day until high school. Right, Milo?"

Ian arrived, and Jess sent him a confused glance. Milo had *never* said a word about knowing Giselle, much less that he had been a close friend of hers. Why had he kept it a secret?

"Like I said," Avery continued, "I might need help with the trunk. Giselle never threw anything away. And it could have books in it."

"She still has stuff here?" Jon asked, frowning. "After all this time?"

Avery nodded. "I've been away, and my dad was too ill to come get it. We arranged to have Mrs. Coates put all of Giselle's stuff in a trunk and keep it for us until I could get here."

"I'll give you a hand," Milo volunteered, and, handing his books to Linda, loped off toward the kitchen and its cellar door.

"I'm sorry about your sister," Jess said as Giselle's brother followed Milo.

Avery McKendrick turned around. "She didn't commit suicide," he said bluntly. "I don't care what you heard, what they told you. She didn't. Not Giselle. It's true that she went through a bad time when our mother became terminally ill. But even on her worst days, Giselle was an optimist." Shaking his head, he added, "My father never believed what they said about her death, and neither do I." He sighed and added, "I just wanted you to know that." Then he left to join Trucker and Milo in the basement.

But when Jess went into the kitchen, Trucker was standing at the refrigerator filling a glass with lemonade.

"I thought you were helping Milo," she said.

"I was. He sent me up here to get some rope."

Upset by her conversation with Avery McKendrick, Jess snapped, "We don't keep the rope in the refrigerator."

Trucker raised dark eyebrows. "That trunk is heavy. Hefting it made me thirsty, okay?"

Jess flushed. "I'm sorry, Trucker. I shouldn't have bitten your head off. I just feel so sorry for Giselle's family."

Trucker nodded. "Yeah. Me, too."

"Forgive me?"

"No problem. Don't worry about it. I'd better get back down there. It's going to take at least two people to haul that trunk out of here."

"Avery's down there, too."

"Good. Three people is even better."

The minute the car had pulled out of the driveway and onto the highway and Trucker had gone back to whatever he'd been working on, Jess turned to Milo. "You *knew* that girl?" she asked. "I can't believe you never said so. That first night, when Ian told us what had happened to her, you never said a word!"

Milo hunched his thin shoulders in a noncommittal shrug. But as he turned to take off for campus, Ian put a hand on his arm. Linda and Jon watched with interest.

"Hey, what gives?" Ian said. "Jess is right. It was pretty weird having that girl's brother talk to you like an old friend."

Milo jerked free of Ian's hand. "I don't make a habit of telling my life story," he said. "And I don't remember anyone else telling *theirs*."

"None of the rest of us," Jess pointed out,

"knew a girl who *died* in this house. But *you* knew her."

"Not in high school, I didn't." Milo's blue eyes behind the wire-framed glasses studied the gravel at his feet. "Her brother was gone by then, so he doesn't know . . ." his voice trailed off. This time, when Milo began walking, Ian didn't try to stop him. But he did grab Jess's hand and follow Milo down the driveway. Linda and Jon came out of the house then and joined them.

"What happened in high school?" Ian asked Milo.

Milo continued walking. "Nothing. She was a big deal. I wasn't. End of story."

"And end of friendship?" Ian's voice was kind.

Milo didn't answer, but Jess had no trouble picturing what had happened. She'd seen it happen to other kids. Best friends in grade school and maybe middle school, sometimes even the first year of high school. Then one person found new friends, new interests, and left the old friend on the outside looking in . . . an awful place to be.

Giselle had been pretty and popular, a "big deal," as Milo put it. And he hadn't.

Sighing, Milo turned to face them, his mouth grim. "Look, this isn't anybody's business but mine, okay? Giselle and I were friends and then we weren't, that's all. I was never her boyfriend. Her boyfriend was some guy from out-of-town. I never met him. Now, can we just forget about this, okay?"

Because Jess felt sorry for him, she nodded. Taking their cue from her, the others did the same. "Old news, Milo," Ian said. "Forgotten."

Milo nodded and said in gruff voice, "Thanks. I mean it, thanks."

But as he turned and resumed his walking, Jess knew she couldn't forget the surprising revelation. Milo hadn't even said how he *felt* about Giselle's death. If they'd been that close, even if it had been a long time ago, he must have been upset by her suicide.

Yet he had shown no emotion of any kind when Ian had told that story during their get-acquainted party on the porch . . . and no emotion when he'd first seen Avery McKendrick standing in the hall waiting to collect Giselle's things.

Weren't poets supposed to be emotional?

Hurrying to class a while later, Jess wished that she could stay forever among the beautiful, red brick and stone buildings covered with ivy, and under the sheltering trees whose leaves were just starting to turn blazing yellows and purples and scarlets. She wished she could stay there forever and never have to return to Nightingale Hall, with all of its unanswered questions.

Chapter 11

In spite of Jess's wish that she could linger on campus indefinitely, the day passed quickly. After attending a brief meeting of the Fall Ball planning committee at the Student Center, she reluctantly returned to Nightingale Hall.

No one else was home. The house was dim and eerily silent. No pipes groaned, no shutters banged, no wild wind shrieked. All three stories of brick sat in silence as if . . . as if the house was waiting for something to happen, Jess thought as she climbed the stairs.

She quickened her steps, eager for her own room, sunnier and brighter than the rest of the house.

But her anticipation died a quick death when she reached the top of the stairs. Staring in dismay, she let out a soft "Oh."

A trail of muddy footprints oozed straight

down the middle of the hall. From one end to the other.

No, that wasn't right. There was something weird . . .

Jess walked the length of the hallway, avoiding the mud, her eyes on the floor. The weird thing about the footprints, she realized, was that they began in the middle of the hall, some distance from where the hallway *began*. They didn't start in a place that made sense, like at the threshold to one of the rooms, as if someone had entered the hallway wearing muddy shoes.

Frowning, she followed the prints to where they curved, suddenly, into . . . *her* room. The muddy footprints ended just inside her door. But when she searched the room with her eyes, she found no one there.

It was as if the person in mud-covered shoes had been dropped from the sky, walked to her room, and then had been snatched skyward again.

Well, that was ridiculous!

Jess studied the oozed prints. Whoever had made such a disgusting mess could, she thought, have slipped out of the muddy shoes when he or she saw what was happening and guiltily carried the shoes back into their bedroom in stocking feet.

But if the shoes had been put *on* in one of the bedrooms, there would be telltale evidence leading from that room. And there wasn't.

And even more disconcerting — why did the footprints lead to her room before they mysteriously stopped?

The front door slammed.

Jess ran to the top of the stairs and called, "Who is it? Ian, is that you?"

"No, it's me, Linda." Footsteps running up the stairs. "And I'm in a rush." Linda came racing up the stairs, her cheeks flushed, her yellow-green hair windblown. "I've got a meet in two hours, and I've got *four* hours of history research to do. Yuck, what's that?" She had reached the top of the stairs, and her mouth turned down in disgust as she surveyed the damage.

"Mud."

"Well, I *know* it's mud." Linda eyed the trail of footprints. "What a mess! Where'd it come from? It hasn't rained lately."

"It's probably always muddy down by the creek." But Jess was trying to figure out how someone could come into the house with muddy shoes but deposit that mud only in the upstairs hall. How had they missed the stairs, and the front hall? "Linda, isn't there something weird about these footprints?"

Linda carefully stepped around the mud. "Weird? Weird how?"

"Well, they start in the middle of the hallway."

Linda shot Jess an exasperated look. "Jess, I really don't have time for this. They're just *footprints*, for pete's sake. Someone slipped a pair of muddy shoes on out in the hall and took them off again when they saw what a mess they were making."

"I thought of that. But then the prints would come from downstairs or out of one of the bedrooms, wouldn't they?"

Linda groaned. "Do we have to make a major case out of this? Listen, Jess, I've got to get busy. I know I should help you clean this up, but I just can't. Don't be mad, okay? Get Trucker to help." She hurried on down the hall and went into her room, closing the door.

This mess doesn't make any sense, Jess thought as she began cleaning it up. She couldn't walk away and leave it there.

But strangest of all, as she scrubbed, it looked like the footprints were fading on their own. The last half-dozen or so clumps of mud seemed to disappear by themselves.

Did mud fade when it dried?

Jess didn't think so.

Strange.

Jess shook her head. Why was she worrying so much about a bunch of footprints? There simply must have been fewer footprints than she'd thought at first, that's all.

When she had finished and the floor was shiny again, she went to her own room to study for a while and maybe take a nap.

Jess awoke with a start, her heart pounding fiercely. How long had she slept? Hours? And what had awakened her?

Faint noises from below told her she wasn't alone in the house. But the noises weren't loud enough to have awakened her. So what had?

Jess lifted her head, her eyes becoming accustomed to the darkness. Had a book fallen from the desk? Had a breeze blown shut her open closet door?

Jess peered into the darkness, exploring . . .

The desk was against the window with everything on it in place as she had left it. The closet door was still slightly ajar. It hadn't slammed shut with a bang.

Then what . . . ?

Something moving on the wall opposite the foot of her bed caught her attention. Something . . . moving . . .

Jess gasped in horror and instinctively yanked the purple bedspread up to her chest in a protective motion. She sat perfectly still, her eyes making round O's of disbelief as she stared in shocked silence.

The wall in front of her moved with the clear, unmistakable shadow of a body swinging back and forth from the light fixture.

Chapter 12

Jess's eyes remained glued to the shadow swinging on the wall opposite the foot of her bed.

The clear outline of long hair, thick and curly, swung out behind the shadowed figure.

Giselle . . . it had to be her. The girl Ian had told them about, the girl Milo knew, the dead sister of Avery McKendrick, the one who had hanged herself in Jess's room.

Jess opened her mouth and screamed, a high, shrill sound that carried out of her room and into the hall.

Trucker, in the kitchen drinking a glass of milk, heard the sound and dropped the cardboard container. Thin, white liquid became a snowy river spreading across the faded linoleum.

Milo, his nose deep in a volume of poetry,

jerked upright on his bed, tilting his head, waiting to see if the sound came again.

Linda, lost in a blissful dream about Milo, was rudely dragged awake by the scream.

Ian, reading at his desk by the window, jumped to his feet and raced to the door, long hair flying out behind him.

Jon had slipped out of the house earlier and was partying at a friend's house.

Cath, exhausted from pulling the all-nighter to rewrite her missing paper, had, like Jess, decided to take a nap. Wrapped cocoonlike in a quilt, she slept blissfully on, hearing nothing.

Ian was the first to arrive in Jess's room. He was followed quickly by Milo and Linda. They found Jess sitting up in bed, scrunched up against the headboard, her eyes squeezed tightly shut. They flew open when Ian arrived and flipped on the light switch.

"What's wrong?" he asked, striding to her bedside.

Without answering, Jess opened her eyes and focused her gaze on the wall. There was nothing there. No swaying shadow. Only tiny sprigs of lilac on a background of white.

The trio gathered around her bed, all wanting to know why she had screamed.

The first thing she said was, "You turned on the light."

Ian nodded. "Right. It was dark in here."

"And it went away."

He leaned over the bed. "What? What went away?"

"*She* did . . . Giselle." Jess couldn't stop shaking.

Linda grabbed the folded quilt from the foot of the bed and draped it around Jess's shoulders. Then she sat down on the bed and asked, "You had a dream about that girl?"

Jess shook her head no. "It wasn't a dream. I woke up and there she was, hanging . . . hanging. . . ." Remembering, her breath caught in her throat and her words died.

Linda glanced up at Milo. "She was dreaming," she said. "Ian," she accused, "you never should have told her about that girl. How would *you* like to go to bed in a room where someone committed suicide? No wonder poor Jess had a nasty nightmare."

"No, I . . . It wasn't a nightmare! It was real." And maybe the scream I heard that first night was real, too."

"Scream?" Ian asked. "What scream?"

"Someone screamed, the first night we

were here. It woke me up. But no one else heard it, so I decided I'd been dreaming. That's why I didn't say anything about it. But now. . ."

No one said anything. But the three exchanged dubious glances.

"And you," Linda scolded Milo, "you shouldn't have made that dumb joke about the house being haunted."

"You're right," he agreed, looking contrite. "I shouldn't have. Sorry, Jess."

"It wasn't a dream," Jess repeated. "Look, turn off the light. You'll see for yourselves."

No one moved.

"Turn it *off* !"

Shaking his head, Ian moved to the light switch. The room returned to total darkness.

Jess stared in disbelief at the bare wall. There was no shadow . . . there was nothing.

"I don't see anything," Ian said, and turned the light back on.

"It was *there*!" Jess cried, tears of frustration stinging her eyelids. "I *saw* it! She had long hair . . . she was hanging there . . ."

"Oh, Jess, don't," Linda said softly. "You'll give us all nightmares. Listen, the best thing to do when you have a bad dream is get up and get really awake, right? That party starts in half an hour, anyway, and you're still going, aren't you? It'll get your mind off your dream."

Jess struggled with the idea that what she had seen was a dream. A dream? But . . .

No, they were right. How could it have been anything else *but* a dream? They all looked so concerned. She was upsetting everyone and making Ian and Milo feel guilty over — *what*? After all, she couldn't *really* have seen that girl hanging in her room, could she? Not a girl who had died last spring. Not possible. So she hadn't heard the scream, either. That, too, was not possible.

She took a deep breath and let it out slowly. Get her mind off it, that was the answer. She had forgotten about the party, but it would be a perfect escape. "Of course I'm going," she said firmly. "Sorry I got everyone all rattled. It was just so *real* . . ."

Linda looked relieved. "Great. You get dressed. Meet you downstairs. Should I wake Cath up? She's napping, too. Her light isn't on."

"No, let her sleep." Jess tossed the quilt aside and stood up. Her jeans looked okay, but her shirt was one giant wrinkle. "She probably wasn't going to the party, anyway."

When Milo and Linda left, Ian stayed behind. He stood over Jess, his dark eyebrows drawn together. "You sure that's what you saw?" he asked. "A shadow of that girl? It couldn't have been a tree branch?"

"Tree branches don't have curly hair, Ian. I must have been wrong about it being real, but I wasn't wrong about whose shadow it was. It was Giselle's."

"Okay. Linda's right. I shouldn't have told you about her. Maybe you could ask Mrs. Coates to switch your room when she gets back."

Right. Like someone else would be willing to sleep in this room now that they all knew the truth.

She knew he was just trying to make her feel better. "Ian," she said as he turned to leave, "Linda wasn't right, blaming you and Milo. Everyone on campus knows about Giselle. I'm glad I heard the story from you first."

"Yeah? You mean it?"

"I mean it. Now get out of here so I can change my clothes."

Five minutes later, Jess left her room. The sense of relief that flooded her as she closed the door behind her made her knees weak. She would have to have such a good time at the party that she'd forget all about Giselle McKendrick. Otherwise, going back into that room when she got home would be impossible.

She did have a good time at the party. But she didn't forget about Giselle.

The party was held in the Student Center on campus.

"This isn't the room where they're holding the Fall Ball," Ian mentioned as they all arrived. "Not big enough. That'll be in the main hall."

But he didn't turn to Jess then and add, "So . . . you want to go with me?" Instead, he smiled at her and moved away to talk to a friend he'd spotted.

Maybe he couldn't afford tickets to the ball. They were expensive. And he'd have to rent a tux and buy a corsage . . .

Maybe *she* should ask *him*.

But you can't afford the tickets, either, she reminded herself. So forget about the ball and have a good time in the here and now. Tonight is *free*.

She met tons of new people. The sophomores hosting the event made it their business to introduce themselves to as many freshmen as possible. Jess met several girls who hinted that she might be considered for their sororities, and she was too polite to tell them she wasn't interested. She met several boys who bragged about their fraternities, and several people who shared her love of music and dancing. She was invited to join the chorus, work on the college newspaper, and volunteer for an adult literacy program conducted in the community by a group of sophomores and juniors.

"I wish I had time for all that," she confided to the tall, heavyset girl with blonde hair who had mentioned the literacy program.

"Well, we hold the sessions right here on campus," the girl, whose name tag read *BETH*, said. She smiled. "You might not even have to leave home. Which dorm are you in?"

Flushing slightly, Jess said, "I'm off-campus. At Nightingale Hall." One of the sorority girls had wrinkled her cute little nose in distaste and disappeared quickly upon receiving this bit of information. Would Beth do the same?

No. She stayed, but a look of sympathy crossed her square, strong face. "Oh." She hesitated, then added, "I guess you know about Giselle, then."

Jess nodded. She didn't want to ask, but she couldn't help herself. "Did you know her?"

"She was in my English lit class," Beth said. "You know, it's strange . . . oh, never mind."

"*What*?" Jess asked. If Beth knew something . . .

"Well, it's just that my last memory of Giselle

is so awful. I . . . I saw her fighting with someone on campus, the day before she died."

"Fighting? You mean arguing?"

"No. *Fighting*. I mean, the other person was yanking on her hair, grabbing her arm, stuff like that."

Jess gasped. "Who was she fighting with?"

Beth shrugged. "I don't know. I was too far away. Couldn't even tell if it was a guy or a girl." She shrugged wide shoulders. "Whoever it was, was wearing jeans and a sweatshirt. Had long hair, though. Dark, I think."

"If you were far away, how could you tell it was Giselle?"

"It was her, all right. I recognized that long, blonde hair." Beth paused, then added, "She was really beautiful. She should have been conceited, but she wasn't. Everyone liked her." Her expression changed, turned bleak. "Well, I guess not *everyone*. Whoever was pushing her around that day sure didn't like her."

"Are you sure they were fighting? I mean, from so far away . . ."

"*That*, I *am* sure of. I started to run to help her, but just then she got away from whoever it was and ran. The other person followed, and I couldn't catch up with them. The next day, she . . . died." Beth shook her head. "None of us could ever figure why she'd do what she did. The last few months of school, she'd changed, become kind of antsy, like she was worried about something. We all thought she was just scared of finals, although she shouldn't have been, she was so bright."

"Did you tell the police about the fight?" Jess asked.

Beth looked surprised. "The police? No, why would I? She committed suicide."

"But . . ."

"Besides, what could I have told them? Like I said, I could never describe the other person. Only . . ." she thought for a minute, then added, "Only, I remember thinking that it wasn't anyone I *knew*. It wasn't anyone I'd ever seen on campus before. I'm not sure why I thought that, but I did."

Then a smiling Ian came to ask Jess to dance, Beth moved away to join friends, and the conversation ended.

Chapter 13

Jess tried to put the conversation with Beth out of her mind. It wasn't, she thought as she leaned her head on Ian's shoulder, as if she'd actually learned anything important.

Except . . . the fight that Beth saw, had taken place on *the day before Giselle died*. Wasn't *that* important?

Someone had been very angry with Giselle McKendrick on the very day before she died.

But . . . she had committed suicide. Everyone said so. The police said so, and it had been in the newspaper.

So what difference did it make whether anyone was mad at her or not?

Concentrating very hard, Jess pushed the unpleasant subject out of her mind. She was surrounded by friends, great music, and a refreshment table so loaded down she expected to hear it groan at any second. And she was where she wanted to be: in Ian Banion's arms.

No more bad thoughts. Not tonight.

On the way home, with a half moon smiling down upon them and Linda and Milo walking several feet ahead, Ian asked Jess, "So, are you going to join me at the *Chronicle*? I know Marty Carr asked you about it. He told me he was going to."

Working with Ian on campus might be fun. She had noticed at the party how many friends he'd already made. Many of them were girls. Had he asked one of *them* to the Fall Ball?

"Maybe. But not until after the ball, because I'm busy with the planning committee." As soon as she'd made the remark, Jess regretted it. Had it sounded like a hint?

If it had, Ian chose to ignore it. Instead, he asked, "Who was the tall blonde girl you were talking to?"

Tall blonde? Oh. Beth. "Beth-something. She knew Giselle." And then, it was strange. Instead of relating to Ian every word of her conversation with Beth, she changed the subject and began asking him about working on the paper.

She had no idea why she did it. She only knew she didn't feel like talking to *anyone* about Giselle. Not even Ian.

Disappointed that he hadn't asked her to the ball, she told him a hasty good-night when they returned to Nightingale Hall, and hurried upstairs.

She had barely closed the door when someone knocked on it. She turned around and pulled it open.

"I forgot something," Ian said. His dark eyes were serious.

"What — " Jess began.

And then she was in Ian's arms and he was kissing her.

It was over much too soon. "Sleep tight," he said and, smiling, turned and went down the hall to his own room.

Jess went to bed certain there would be no bad dreams that night.

The next day, Jess found herself looking for Beth as she made her way across campus between classes. The day was clear and unseasonably warm, the sun bright. There were things Jess wanted to know about the girl who had lived in the lilac bedroom last spring. And . . . died there. Maybe Beth could fill her in.

But while she saw many other people from the party, all of whom waved, smiled and said,

"Hi, Jess," she didn't catch a glimpse of the tall, heavyset girl.

Maybe, she told herself on the way home, it was just as well. She shouldn't be thinking about Giselle. It had all happened months ago, and had nothing to do with her. Putting it out of her mind should put an end to shadows on her wall.

She had barely seen Ian all day, and when she did, she felt awkward. He had kissed her. But he *hadn't* asked her to the ball. Confusing. Very confusing.

Go figure, she told herself.

She had been studying for almost an hour when she heard hurried footsteps on the stairs and in the hall, followed by the slamming of a door. Someone else had come home. Good. After sharing an apartment with three other people, she still felt uneasy being in the huge old house all alone, even when Trucker was working nearby.

After all, hadn't someone entered Cath's room without her permission? Maybe being alone at Nightingale Hall wasn't such a hot idea.

Her relief lasted all of two minutes. It ended when a shriek filled the air, bringing her out of her chair and running to the door.

The sound came again when she was in the hall. It came from Linda's room. Jess didn't even bother to knock when she got there. She burst into the room and found Linda standing in front of her chest of drawers, her cheeks scarlet with fury, her eyes blazing. She was waving something in the air.

"I don't *believe* this!" she shouted. "I've got a meet in thirty minutes and look what someone did to my suit!" Using both hands, she waved half a dozen bright blue latex strips in Jess's face.

Jess realized immediately what the strips were. Or *had* been. Linda's bathing suit. The blue one-piece with the Salem University seal across the left hip. Although freshman swim team members could wear any suit they chose to practices, the university suit was required for meets.

"Why would someone *do* this to me?" Linda wailed. And then her face crumpled and she added in almost a whisper, her eyes wide with horror, "Jess . . . this means that someone came into my room when I wasn't here."

Jess shoved aside the thought of someone sneaking into Linda's room, unwilling to deal with the ugliness of it, and said, "Don't you have another suit?"

"I couldn't afford two!" Fresh tears flowed. "The other girls all have an extra, but I don't. They're expensive."

Cath, Milo, and Trucker suddenly appeared in the doorway. "What's going on?" Trucker asked.

Jess explained.

Cath stepped forward to examine the destruction. "Well," she said as she stepped back again, "now you know how *I* felt when my paper disappeared. And that paper was a lot more important than some stupid swim meet."

"That stupid swim meet," Linda said vehemently, "is why I have my scholarship! Your mommy and daddy dearest may have handed *you* a college education on a silver platter, but mine couldn't." Linda's hand, clutching the bathing suit tatters, shook. "I've worked my buns off since high school to make a college team. Now I have to miss an important meet because some creep went crazy with a pair of scissors. If we miss a meet for any reason other than *death*, we're out of the next meet. So I'll miss two! Coach is going to be furious." She glared at Cath with reddened eyes. "What do you think missing two meets is going to do to my chances of having my scholarship renewed next semester? If it's not renewed, I'll have to leave school."

To Jess's astonishment, Milo moved forward then to put a sympathetic arm around Linda's shoulders. Grateful for the support, Linda managed a wan smile.

But a moment later, she pulled away and turned to face Cath. "You did this, didn't you?" she whispered harshly. "To get even with me for sticking up for Milo about that dumb essay. You *witch!*"

"That's stupid," Cath retorted, her cheeks flushing with anger. "I never went into your room. I came straight home from school and never left my room."

"I didn't even know you were home," Jess interjected in surprise. "It was so quiet here, I thought I was the only one home."

"Cath's right, though," Trucker said. "I was changing light bulbs out in the hall and I saw her come in." He glanced at Jess. "Must have been right after you got here. I was putting the ladder away when Linda yelled, but I'd been in the hall that whole time and I never saw Cath leave her room."

Linda whirled and went to the window. It was wide open. "You mean, she never came out into the *hall*. But the fire escape is right outside this window. And right outside *her* window, next door. She could easily have climbed out of her room and into mine without anyone seeing her."

"Oh, please," Cath said, "I don't go around climbing in and out of windows. You probably slashed that bathing suit yourself so you could accuse *me*. Because *I* accused your precious Milo. The difference is, *he's* guilty. *I'm* not." She turned and headed for the door. Over her shoulder, she said, "You should be relieved, Linda. Those suits are the ugliest things I've ever seen. Even on people with *good* figures." Then she left the room, with a toss of her hair.

But a furious Linda wasn't ready to drop the matter. "Come on!" she urged Milo, Jess, and Trucker as Cath, her back as rigid as a flagpole, left the room, "I want to check out Cath's windows. Maybe she left footprints on the fire escape or something . . ."

"Linda, don't be ridiculous," Jess said, hoping to avoid any more confrontations.

But Linda was already out of the room. A second later, she was pounding on Cath's closed door. "Let us in," she shouted, "or I'll make Trucker remove this door!"

An annoyed Cath let them in.

It was unbearably hot in the small, immaculate room. Linda rushed to the window.

"It won't open," Cath said, an amused smile on her face. "Go ahead, try it. It's been stuck since last night. You'll see that I couldn't have got out that way even if I'd wanted to, which I didn't." Fixing dark eyes on Linda's back, she added, "Actually, I thought maybe some malicious person had *glued* it shut, hoping I'd suffocate in this heat."

Trucker moved toward the window. "It's probably the humidity. Let me try." He reached Linda and placed his hands on the window frame.

The window slid up as easily as if it had been greased.

Silence dropped into the room like a bomb. All eyes moved to Cath.

Her face was a vivid, painful red. "But I . . . I . . ." she stammered, "I wrestled with that window *forever* last night." Her eyes went to Jess in an appeal for support. "Would I be studying in an oven if I could have opened that window?"

"Did you try it when you got home today?" Trucker asked.

"No. I thought it wouldn't do any good. I tried it last night and again this morning, and it wouldn't budge. I was going to ask you to fix it after school, but you were busy with the light bulbs. I thought I'd wait until you were done."

"Oh, brother," Linda groaned, "is anybody buying this?"

"Linda," Jess said quickly, "you're going to be late for the meet. I'm sure you can borrow a suit from one of the other swimmers." Firmly taking Linda's arm, Jess began leading the way out of the room. "You won't miss this meet *or* the next one, and your scholarship is perfectly safe."

Linda went with Jess, but she was still angry. "If she thinks I'm going to forget about this," she muttered, "she's crazy." And when they reached her room, Linda turned to Jess and said, "Thanks, Jess, for getting me away from Cath before I totally lost my cool." She opened the door. "But . . . listen, be careful, okay?" Her round pink face was very serious. "This time, it was only a bathing suit. But next time, who knows?"

The warning rang in Jess's ears as she returned to Cath's room.

Chapter 14

In Cath's room, Trucker was still checking the window frame.

"I'm telling you," Cath was saying in a low, intense voice, "I couldn't *open* it!"

Already convinced that Cath hadn't been traveling back and forth via the fire escape, Jess focused on the awful truth: someone had trespassed in both Cath's room and Linda's. That was scary.

The doors to their rooms all had locks, but because only six students were living in the house, they'd never felt the need to use the locks. Until now.

"Trucker, do you know if the keys to our rooms are still around somewhere?" Jess asked.

He shook his head. "Not likely. Probably haven't been used in years. But I can look around."

"Well, if you don't find them," Cath said, "get

us new locks, okay? I'm not staying in this room any longer without a lock on the door."

Trucker looked doubtful. "New locks? That'd be expensive. I'd have to check with Mrs. Coates."

Cath looked crestfallen. "I wish you would all just leave," she said in a defeated voice. "I *didn't* climb out any window, I was never on the fire escape, and I didn't touch Linda's bathing suit." Her voice began to quaver. "And I think it's really rotten that you would think I'd do those things."

"*I* don't," Jess said. "I don't think that, Cath."

"And I didn't take your essay, either," Milo said. "It's no fun being unfairly accused, is it?" He turned and left the room.

Jess was lost in thought as she returned to her own room.

Jon was on the phone in the hall, his chair tilted back against the wall, a grin on his face.

Talking to a girl, of course, Jess thought, realizing that Jon probably knew nothing about the bathing suit episode. He must have just arrived home and had gone, naturally, straight to the telephone.

"Look," he said into the phone as Jess passed, "what can I say? Blue-eyed blondes make me weak in the knees. Pick you up at seven tomorrow night, okay?"

Jess rolled her eyes heavenward and went on into her room. Cath wasn't blonde and blue-eyed, and Jon flirted with her constantly. He should have said, *"Females* make me weak in the knees." That would be closer to the truth.

She had begun keeping a sweater on the inside doorknob of her room, automatically shrugging into its warmth every time she entered. That done, she went to her desk and stood looking out the window into darkness. The fire escape was out there, winding its way up from the ground. Could someone be using it to get into their rooms?

Who would do that?

And *why*? To steal an essay, shred a bathing suit? That made no sense. If those things had happened to only one person, say, to Cath, it would look like someone was angry with her and acting out that anger. But *both* girls' belongings had been vandalized.

And maybe the person who had committed those acts of vandalism wasn't *finished*. If he could get into Cath's and Linda's rooms, he could get into anyone's.

Trucker had better find those keys.

Then Jess laughed aloud, the sound echoing

hollowly in her room. Keys? Where was her mind? If the vandal was using the fire escape and the windows, what good would door keys do?

Still, locking the doors might make them *feel* safer.

To take her mind off questions she couldn't answer, she went back out into the hall. Jon was still on the telephone.

"Your lips are going to fall off," she told him sternly. "Let someone else have a crack at the phone for a change."

He put his hand over the mouthpiece. "Is it an emergency?" he asked with an impish grin. "Do you need to call an ambulance, the police, or the fire department?"

"You're going to *need* an ambulance if you don't get off the phone," Jess threatened. "Come on, Jon, didn't anyone ever teach you to share?"

"Sharing is for kids. And I never did get the hang of it." But he relented then. He whispered something into the phone and hung up. "You realize you could be wrecking my entire social life," he said.

"It would take an act of Congress to wreck *your* social life," Jess said curtly.

Laughing, Jon departed.

*   *   *

Another week passed without an invitation
from Ian to the Fall Ball. Attending the planning committee meetings was hard for Jess,
knowing she might not even be going. She
fought to put that depressing thought behind
her and concentrate on the task at hand.

As fall approached, Twin Falls was struck
with one last summer heat wave. The temper-
ature climbed steadily throughout the day. By
the time Jess left campus, she was sweltering
in her gray sweatshirt. Thoughts of slipping
into one of her cool, short-sleeved T-shirts
quickened her steps back to Nightingale Hall.

Jess ran lightly up the wide stone steps and
into the house. It was dim, cool — thanks to
the heavy draperies — and smelled faintly of
burned toast.

Again she felt the strong sensation that the
house was waiting for something.

Silly, silly. It was just a house.

Upstairs in her room, she hurried to the
squat, ugly, old-fashioned chest of drawers
against one wall. Crouching, she pulled the bottom drawer open. Her T-shirts should have
been lying on top. But they weren't. Instead,
three heavy sweaters, their long sleeves tossed
awry, met her reaching fingers.

That was odd. She distinctly remembered placing all warmer clothing at the very bottom of the drawer, her T-shirts readily accessible on top. When cold weather arrived to stay, she had planned to reverse the layers.

But she was positive she hadn't done that yet.

Then . . . why weren't her T-shirts where she'd put them?

Uneasiness crept upon her. Had someone been in her room, too? Going through her things?

The thought made her sick.

So far, nothing was damaged. Maybe she had switched the layers, and forgotten.

Her fingers began a search for the submerged T-shirts. Probing beneath the layers of sweaters and sweatshirts in the wide, deep drawer, her hand brushed up against something that didn't feel like fabric. Instead of soft, cool cotton, she was touching something warm and smooth . . . and it felt like it was . . . moving!

Jess jerked her arm backward so fast, she cracked her elbow sharply against the drawer front. Yelping in pain, she reached with her left hand to comfort the wounded arm . . . and her fingers again touched wet warmth. Thinking she might be bleeding, her eyes darted to the elbow in search of bright, oozing red.

There was no red. There was pink, and lots of it, and the skin on her arm seemed to be alive . . .

From the back of her hand to just below her elbow, her flesh was thick with fat, pink, moist, wriggling . . .

Worms.

Chapter 15

The sound that came from Jess's mouth at the sight of her flesh crawling with fat, pink worms wasn't a scream. It was a low, horrified moan of disbelief. She batted frantically at the repulsive creatures, flicking them from her skin onto the hardwood floor, where they lay, stunned. The floor writhed with pink.

Trembling, rubbing her arms to erase the feel of crawling flesh, she stared down at the drawer. She couldn't bear the thought of putting her hands in there again. But . . . she had to make sure there were no more creatures.

She despised slithery things: snakes, lizards, crawly creatures. She had never understood how anyone could actually pick up one of the slimy things to bait a fishing hook. Yet Ian, Milo, and Trucker did it all the time. Gross!

Slowly, carefully, scarcely breathing, Jess peeled aside the top layer of sweaters.

Nothing.

Breathing shallowly, she dug deeper, beyond the second layer, her sweatshirts.

Still nothing. Only soft, worn fabric. Nothing warm and moist and slimy.

Carefully, gingerly, she removed, in two separate stacks, the bottom layer of T-shirts.

And stared in openmouthed horror.

The bottom of her dresser drawer was a teeming mass of slithering pink.

She screamed.

Outside, a startled Trucker dropped his hammer and ran for the porch steps.

Ian, reaching the top of the hill on his way home, saw Trucker race for the house. Sensing trouble, he broke into a run.

When Trucker burst into Jess's room, he found her kneeling on the floor in front of her dresser. She was white-faced and silent, rocking back and forth, her arms wound around her chest.

Ian was right behind Trucker. In simultaneous strides, they reached Jess. "What?" Ian demanded, kneeling. When his eyes followed Jess's glazed stare, he let out a soft whistle.

"Oh, man," he moaned, and folded Jess into his chest, hiding her face in his shoulder, "you poor kid."

"They must have come up from the cellar," Trucker said crouching to get a better look. "Maybe through the chimney? Geez, Jess, I'm sorry!"

Jess lifted her head. From the cellar? So many worms? No. "Someone *put* them there," she said, her voice amazingly calm.

Ian stared down at her. "You saw someone in your room?"

She shook her head. "No." But Cath hadn't seen anyone in *her* room, either, or Linda in hers. "People who do disgusting things like this don't *let* themselves be seen. They're too sneaky. But someone was in here. There are too many worms for this to be accidental."

"I'll get rid of this mess for you," Trucker volunteered. "I'll take it out back and dump it." Using a piece of folded paper, he collected the worms Jess had knocked off her arm and slid them into the drawer.

It was too heavy and awkward for one person to carry. Although Trucker was accustomed to lifting weighty loads, his back and shoulder muscles strained against his white overalls when he attempted to lift the drawer.

"Ian, help him!" Jess urged.

"I'm not leaving you up here alone. You look like you're going to be sick."

"I'm not going to be sick. I'm fine. Just help Trucker, okay?" Her voice rose. "I want that drawer *out* of here. Toss the clothes in the laundry in the kitchen, okay? I'll wash them later." The thought of wearing anything that had been in the drawer made her sick. But she couldn't afford a whole new wardrobe.

She stood up. Her legs proved unreliable, so she moved to the bed and sat down. "Go on. Please, Ian. Help Trucker."

Reluctantly, Ian took one end of the drawer while Trucker moved to the other end.

When they had taken the drawer out, Jess sank back against the pillows. Her body felt leaden, and her head ached from restraining tears she had refused to shed.

Was she overreacting? Could the worms have been someone's idea of a practical joke? Who would think something that disgusting was funny?

Milo, Trucker, and Ian all fished. They were used to handling worms. Would one of them think dumping a bunch of worms in someone's drawer was a great gag?

She couldn't believe that *anyone* in the house would find any humor in something so revolting.

But if it wasn't a joke . . . then what *was* it?

A scare tactic? She had certainly *been* scared.

Why would someone want to frighten her?

Joke or scare tactic, someone had been in her room. Someone had touched her things. Someone had come in and out, leaving a repulsive message behind.

Trucker *had* to find those keys. Or put new locks on their doors. This couldn't keep happening. How could any of them feel safe?

She got up when Trucker and Ian returned with the empty drawer. "We hosed it down and dried it," Trucker told Jess in a comforting voice. Ian removed a handful of papers that had slid underneath the chest and then they pushed the drawer back into place.

It looks like nothing happened in here, Jess thought. Anyone who walked in now would never guess I was totally freaked-out fifteen minutes ago.

"Thanks, guys," Jess said weakly. "I couldn't have lifted that drawer by myself." After a moment, she added, "Look, how about if we keep this to ourselves, okay? I don't want people giving me weird looks at dinner. It was probably just a joke, anyway."

And even though no one in the room believed that for a second, Trucker and Ian nodded. But their faces were glum.

"Listen, let's not cook tonight," she said, desperately needing to get out of her room and out of Nightingale Hall. "We deserve a treat, after what we just went through. There's Hunan Manor, the Chinese place in town. How about it, guys?" She knew she was talking too fast and too loud, but she couldn't help it. She was in a hurry to escape.

"Sure," Ian said, putting his arm around Jess, "great idea!" He hesitated, then added, "Trucker, you up for Chinese?"

"Sounds great." Then Trucker looked from Jess to Ian and back to Jess again. He shrugged. "But . . . too much to do."

Jess smiled at him. Very perceptive guy.

Ian tried, and failed, to look disappointed. "Oh, well, sure. Next time, right?" Turning to Jess, he said, "Well, looks like it's just you and me, kid. You ready?"

"What about everyone else?" she asked. "Shouldn't we see if the others are home and want to go?"

"No, we shouldn't." Ian's voice was firm. "They're on their own tonight!"

Jess was amazed to find that she was laughing as they left Nightingale Hall.

To Jess's disappointment, they weren't alone at the restaurant very long. Ian had made many friends on campus and Jess, too, was collecting new friends rapidly. In a short time, their table was crowded, with people pulling up chairs and squeezing in. The table filled up with food, which rapidly disappeared and was just as rapidly replaced with more dishes and platters.

It was crowded, noisy, and hot, but Jess found all of it comforting after the afternoon's horror.

And she still had the walk home with Ian to look forward to.

Home . . . the walk there was the *only* part she was looking forward to. The thought of actually being back inside Nightingale Hall, in that room, with that chest of drawers, made her stomach churn.

Had Trucker collected every single one of the worms she'd slapped from her arm? What if one or two of them had slipped under her chest of drawers and hidden there?

Telling herself that she or Trucker or Ian would have spotted them, she returned her attention to the table.

"So, how's life at Nightmare Hall?" a small, red-haired girl named Tina asked Ian. "Are you ready now to join the real world and move into an on-campus dorm?" Her lips curled in a coy smile. "We'd be glad to have you."

I'll just bet you would, Jess thought.

"It's not that bad," Ian said, avoiding Jess's eyes. "The place sort of grows on you."

The girl laughed. "Like fungus?"

"And the fishing's great."

"Ugh! Fishing? Boring! Sitting around putting worms on hooks is *not* my idea of a good time."

A vision of the mass of moist, pink, creepy-crawling creatures slammed back into Jess's mind so hard, her eyes closed and she was forced to lean back in her chair.

"Hey, you okay?" Ian grabbed for her hand.

"I need air." And *lots* of it.

"Right. Let's go." There were protests from their friends, but Ian had thrown some money on the table and was already gently moving Jess to the door.

"Those girls at the table won't invite me to join *their* sorority," Jess joked weakly as they began the walk home. "They hate me for taking you away."

Ian laughed. "A minor loss. They'll get over it."

I'm not sure *I* would, she thought, and was surprised. She really didn't know him all that well. Since when did Jess-The-Cautious fall for someone she hardly knew?

That's ridiculous, she corrected herself. I haven't *fallen* for anyone.

He didn't ask her what had upset her back in the restaurant. She guessed that he'd figured it out and didn't want to bring up the subject again. Good thinking.

Instead, they talked about living away from home for the first time. Everyone at Nightingale Hall came from small towns around the area and could have, had they chosen to, made the trip back home in a couple of hours. It wasn't as if they'd moved across the country.

"But we're still on our own," Ian said, "even if our folks aren't that far away. I bummed around some last summer. Hopped on my Harley and went exploring. It was fun, and it showed me I could take care of myself."

No wonder he seemed older, more self-confident than everyone else at Nightingale Hall. It wasn't just his height or build or his long hair. It was because he'd already been on his own for a little while.

Jess was reluctant to go inside when they reached Nightingale Hall. Sensing her feelings, Ian sat down on the top step and pulled her down beside him.

Jess snuggled against his chest when he put an arm around her. She certainly wasn't ready to go back to her room. Maybe she'd *never* be ready. Maybe she'd have to spend the rest of the year on the front porch.

If Ian would stay out here with her . . .

That seemed like an even better idea when he bent his head to kiss her.

Chapter 16

Ian peeled carrots at the sink the following night while Jess heated the huge pan of lasagna Maddie Carthew had brought, and Jon and Cath set the table. Milo returned from fishing with Trucker in tow.

So far, Trucker had had no luck finding keys for their doors.

Watching Ian work, Jess remembered the slimy pink creatures in her dresser drawer. A mental picture of Ian, a fishing pole over his shoulder, disappearing into the woods carrying a coffee-can filled with bait came, unbidden, into her mind. Then his face was replaced by Trucker's, and then Milo's.

No. Not them. They wouldn't. The vandal didn't have to be a fisherman, anyway. Maybe he'd just wanted it to *look* like one of them had done it.

Jess couldn't stand suspecting Ian. Remembering his kisses, she shivered with pleasure and quickly moved to the refrigerator to collect lettuce and tomatoes. She'd much rather concentrate on the kisses. But the suspicions kept popping into her mind.

She stood at the open refrigerator door for a long time, lost in thought.

"You're wise to keep an eye on it," Ian said as he joined her. "Never can tell about large appliances. Sometimes they take off without a moment's notice."

When she failed to laugh, he frowned. "Hey, kiddo," he said in a low voice, "what's up? Did I *do* something? Peel the carrots wrong? How many ways can there be to peel carrots?"

She was saved from answering by an impromptu game of catch between Jon and Milo, in which a loaf of French bread was the ball. Milo missed. The long, foil-wrapped loaf hit Ian in the small of the back and, their conversation forgotten, he whirled to join the game.

When she carried the steaming lasagna to the table, Jess had to maneuver around the ballplayers, still cavorting with the French bread. Linda came in, laughed at their antics, and went over to Jess. "Milo and I are going to the library together tonight," she confided in a low voice. "What should I wear?"

The bread sailed past them, caught by Jon at the opposite end of the kitchen. "Touchdown!" he shouted in triumph.

"What should you wear to the *library*?" Jess asked. "Well, spike heels, definitely, and if you have any diamond earrings, wear those and . . ."

"Jess!" Linda laughed. "Come on, be serious."

The bread escaped from Trucker's grasping hands and thunked into a large white ceramic goose stationed on top of the refrigerator. It toppled sideways and landed on its side with a clang.

"Okay, guys, cut it out!" Cath scolded sharply.

Jess sighed. Everyone else seemed more relaxed, but Cath was still strung tighter than a violin. She wasn't eating much, and Jess suspected that she wasn't sleeping, either. She certainly *looked* like she hadn't been sleeping. There were dark circles under her eyes.

It wasn't as if Jess didn't understand how Cath felt. Cath's privacy had been invaded, and Jess knew, now, what that felt like. It was horrible.

But Cath was letting it make her crazy. Ruining her first year at college. She looked like she might fall apart at any second.

"You'll wreck something," Cath told Milo. "Mrs. Coates has a lot of antique pieces in this house."

"Yeah, right," Milo said, sinking into a chair. "Antiques, spelled J-U-N-K."

Cath sniffed. "I thought poets were supposed to appreciate the finer things in life."

"I appreciate the finer things enough to know that stupid goose isn't one of them."

Jess found herself wishing that Cath would call a truce with Linda and Milo. Everyone else seemed to be getting along well, in spite of the tension caused by the stories of Giselle's death and the recent vandalism. But it was obvious that Cath hadn't forgiven Milo for the stolen essay, and equally obvious that Linda and Milo were on edge around Cath.

Remembering Ian's quote about standing together, Jess thought, we should all be united now, trying to find out what's going on around here. The vandalism involves everyone, even those people whose rooms haven't been invaded yet. Because they still could be. We don't have any reason to think that it's over.

After dinner, Linda helped load the dishwasher. "I didn't know Milo ever *went* to the library," Jess said. "Are you sure he'll know how to behave?"

Linda laughed and said, "Of *course* he will. Milo is a *poet*, Jess. He's probably spent hours in libraries."

"I still have trouble with the fact that Milo lied about knowing Giselle." Jess knew the statement might rile Linda, but she had to say it. True, Milo *had* explained why he hadn't mentioned knowing Giselle. And it made sense. But it still rankled that he hadn't told them he'd known her.

"He *didn't* lie. No one *asked* him if he knew her."

"But he never volunteered the information. That's almost the same thing. Even when Ian told us what happened to her, Milo never said a word."

Linda's cheeks reddened, and she was about to answer when Milo and Ian returned from hauling the trash to the bottom of the hill.

Jess had learned nothing.

When she went upstairs and passed Linda's room, she found Linda's door open. Linda was inside, primping in front of her dresser mirror in preparation for her library "date" with Milo.

"You've done a super job with your room,"

Jess said from the doorway. "I love that bed-spread." It was splashed with brilliant flowers in vivid shades of red.

Linda flushed with pleasure. "Oh, thanks. Come on in. Maybe you can help me tame my hair. My grandmother sent me the spread when I told her my room was plain old white. It helps, right?"

"It sure does." So did the seascape posters and high school pennants Linda had tacked on the walls. Her bookshelves were crammed with swimming trophies, and a photo gallery of her family and friends had been taped to the thick wooden frame around her dresser mirror.

Linda's eyes were bright with excitement. Jess couldn't help asking, "Linda, are you sure Milo sees this library thing as a date?"

Hairbrush in hand, Linda turned away from the mirror to face Jess. "Look," she said, nervously fingering the collar of her peacock blue blouse, "I know you think I'm being really dippy about Milo. But . . . I never dated in high school. I mean *never*. Not once."

Jess looked at her inquiringly. "But . . ."

"I'm a *big* girl, Jess. Bigger than most of the guys in my high school. The ones who did tower over me were jocks and they weren't keen on dating a hotshot girl athlete." She said the last with difficulty, letting Jess know the pain was still fresh. Putting on her earrings, Linda added wistfully, "My parents were always so proud of their daughter-the-athlete. They never guessed I was lying awake nights wishing I had a date. And," her round face flushed more deeply, "feeling ashamed because I wanted something so . . . trivial."

"Everyone wants to go out and have fun," Jess said. "That's not anything to be ashamed of."

Linda slid her feet into black flats. "Well, Milo's no jock, that's for sure. Maybe that's why he appeals to me. Besides," she added with the smallest of grins, "he's taller than me. I could even wear heels." Her grin widened. "Even spike heels."

Jess laughed. "You look really pretty," she said sincerely. "And forget about not dating in high school. I mean, look at someone like Giselle McKendrick. Everyone says she was so popular. She probably dated a lot. But it didn't make *her* happy, or she wouldn't have done what she did."

"Yeah, I guess you're right. Suicide," Linda sighed, and bent over to adjust her shoe.

The word "suicide" had barely left her mouth when there was a sharp, cracking sound from the mirror behind her.

And then, as Jess watched in horror from her seat on the bed, the wide square of glass exploded outward into a thousand pieces.

Chapter 17

The mirror exploded with such force, the chunks and shards and slivers of glass were propelled far out into the room, like arrows shot from a bow. It was that very force that saved Jess, who sat on the foot of the bed, directly in the line of fire. The glass arrows were flung over her head and beyond her, to pierce the pillows, stab the wall pennants and posters, and dive into the floor near the head of the bed.

Linda, her eyes wide with terror, remained frozen in a crouched position.

"Oh, God," she breathed when the last piece of shattered glass had clinked to the floor, "what was *that*?"

Jess, her face hidden behind her hands, whispered, "Is it over?"

Linda straightened up cautiously. Her face was as white as the wall behind her. "I think so." She glanced at her dresser. "My mirror is gone." There was awe in her voice. "Totally gone!"

The explosion had been heard by the others. Feet ran down the hall, someone pounded on the door. "Linda?" It was Milo. "What was *that*?"

"The mirror attacked us," Linda said without emotion, as if she couldn't believe it herself. "Watch out for glass on the floor."

Ian was right behind Milo. He went to Jess, sat down next to her. "You're not hurt?"

She shook her head. A tiny piece of glass fell from her hair to the bedspread. She slid her hands away from her face, checking quickly for cuts. She found only one small scratch on her left hand, another on her right forearm. She saw none on Linda.

"What *happened*?" Cath cried as she entered the room. She was wrapped in a long yellow robe, her hair clustered into a careless ponytail. "You broke your mirror?"

"I didn't *break* it," Linda said, leaning against Milo. He put an arm around her and she sent him a grateful look. "*It* broke. By it-self. It . . . exploded."

Jess nodded. "That's exactly what happened.

I know it sounds crazy, but no one did anything to it. Linda bent to fix her shoe and the mirror exploded."

"If I hadn't," Linda interrupted, pressing a fist to her mouth, "if I hadn't bent over . . ." the thought was too horrible to finish and she fell silent.

Jess finished the thought in her head. If Linda hadn't been bending over, she could have been sliced to ribbons by all that flying glass.

Cath sank down on the bed, next to Ian. "Mirrors don't just . . . explode." She looked to Ian for confirmation. "Do they?"

They're not *supposed* to, Jess thought as Ian shrugged. But then, lots of things happen in this house that aren't supposed to.

Trucker appeared in the doorway. "What a mess! Somebody throw a rock through the window?"

Jess hadn't thought of that. The window *was* open, and had no screen. Maybe some neighborhood kid had been practicing his pitching skills?

"I didn't see a rock. Did you, Linda?"

Linda shook her head. "I didn't see a thing. I heard a crack, that's all." She looked doubtful. "I guess something *could* have hit the mirror."

When they had carefully cleaned up the

glass, they all searched under the furniture for some object that might have made the mirror its target. They found nothing.

But because something thrown from outside was the only explanation that seemed to make sense, they all agreed that they simply weren't looking in the right places, that whatever had hit the mirror was almost certainly somewhere in the room.

It wasn't until they were leaving, toting brown grocery sacks filled with broken glass, that Jess remembered what she and Linda had been talking about when the mirror exploded. Giselle . . . they'd been talking about Giselle's suicide.

And she remembered the first time that topic had been mentioned, in Ian's story on the front porch that first night. An upstairs window had suddenly slammed shut. Then they'd gone inside to the kitchen. And as they'd talked about the incident a little more, the light had gone out abruptly. And now, tonight, Linda had mentioned the word "suicide," and the mirror had exploded.

The thought that there might be a connection was so off-the-wall and made so little sense, that Jess dismissed it as too, *too* weird.

But even as everyone was repeating how

lucky the two girls had been, escaping serious injury, an uneasiness settled over her and she knew that it wouldn't go away until she left the house.

So Ian had no trouble persuading her to go see a movie on campus. Jess jumped at the chance to get away from the house.

I would have *seen* something coming through the window in Linda's room, she thought as she collected a jacket and her campus I.D. I *would* have.

Cath surprised everyone by deciding to go to the movie, too, adding, "*I'm* not staying here alone." Linda and Milo agreed to go on to the library.

And Jess decided that pretending that everything was normal was much better than acknowledging the waves of uneasiness that crawled up her spine like ants. And as long as they were out of the house, she *could* pretend.

The movie was hilarious, and Ian held her hand the whole time. Feeling completely safe in the crowded campus theater, Jess relaxed and laughed, forgetting her uneasiness.

After the movie, Trucker drove them into town for pizza. Vinnie's, which served the best pizza in town, was mobbed. Jess saw Jon in a corner booth, a ponytailed blonde seated next to him. Remembering Jon's telephone conversation she knew, without checking, that the girl's eyes had to be blue.

Spotting Jon, Cath deliberately turned to Trucker and began chatting animatedly, as if she had, at that very moment, suddenly realized how attractive he was.

Jess hid a smile. Cath says she's not interested in Jon, she thought to herself, but if she's not at this very moment trying to make him jealous, then I'm a pizza-hater.

She hoped Trucker wouldn't take Cath's flirting seriously. It would be a mistake. While the others accepted Trucker as a friend, Cath still snobbishly saw him as "the handyman." She would never seriously consider him a potential boyfriend.

Although Jess had a good time, she found herself missing Linda and Milo. She was so surprised by the fact, she mentioned it to Ian.

He nodded. "Yeah, me, too. Maybe that means the residents of Nightingale Hall are starting to come together as a group, right?"

Cath and Trucker had gone to the jukebox to make selections, so Jess felt free to say, "I know Cath hasn't forgiven Milo for the essay she thinks he stole. But at least they're speaking to each other. That's a beginning, right?"

But her optimism began to dwindle the minute they left the restaurant. And by the time they drove up the gravel driveway, it had completely disappeared, and dread had taken its place.

She stared up at Nightingale Hall and knew she didn't want to go inside.

It wasn't a safe place to be.

She would have felt silly saying so. No one had seen the shadow on her wall or heard the scream. Linda's shredded bathing suit had been forgotten, and the shattered mirror was being attributed to an object being tossed through the window by a neighborhood kid.

So, everyone else jumped out of the truck and walked into the house as if it were an ordinary dorm, where ordinary things happened.

And Jess followed, because although she was almost sure now that Nightingale Hall wasn't the least bit ordinary, there didn't seem to be any other choice.

In her room, Jess found she was too unsettled to sleep. Wrapping the quilt around her shoulders and switching on her bedside lamp, she grabbed a pile of papers from her desk and sat on the bed intending to sort them out until she felt sleepy.

History essay, math assignment, notice

about overdue library books, a letter from her sister Nell, a photograph . . .

Jess's hand paused in midair.

The photograph wasn't hers. She had never seen it before.

It was dusty. She wiped it off with an edge of the quilt, and as she did, she remembered Ian pulling several pieces of paper from underneath the chest of drawers. This picture must have been one of them.

Leaning back against the headboard, she held the small, square, colored photograph closer to the blue lamp on her nightstand.

There was something very wrong with the picture.

The girl whose head and shoulders filled the square space was very pretty. Her hair was thick, shoulder-length, and very blonde, her bright blue eyes clear, her skin smooth, her face oval. She could easily, Jess thought, be considered gorgeous.

But across her face, someone had drawn a nasty, thick black slash.

Who was this girl?

Who was she kidding? She knew perfectly well who it was. She knew as well as she knew her own name that the girl in the photograph was Giselle McKendrick.

Chapter 18

Staring down at the photograph, Jess realized she'd seen the face before. But where?

Then she remembered. In the photo booth, at the arcade. The face she was looking at now was the same face in the "double exposure" on their strip of film.

Giselle had been in their photo? How could that be?

A violent shudder seized Jess, and she wrapped the quilt more tightly around her shoulders. Tearing her gaze away from the photo, she glanced down at the pile of papers in her lap. Ian had unearthed more than one paper from under the chest. What else had been hiding under that bottom drawer? Did she really want to know?

There was a sheet of paper, letter-size. No envelope. The paper was white, unlined, a trace of gossamer cobweb clinging to its upper right-hand corner. It had been folded twice, and the creases remained.

The typewritten words had faded. But they were legible.

Dear Giselle, Jess read, and with a sharp intake of breath, she closed her eyes, letting the letter fall.

But she knew she had to read it.

She sank back against the pillows and read:

Dear Giselle,
Your time has run out. You've stalled long enough. You haven't answered any of my phone calls or my letters. So I'm coming there and you'd better be ready to leave with me. I'm not taking no for an answer.

The letter was signed, *Your Forever Love*.

But it didn't sound very loving.

Jess gripped the sheet of paper in her fist. Its angry message repeated itself in her head. What did it mean? The writer intended to come to campus, that was clear enough. To get Giselle and take her somewhere . . . and he sounded very, very angry.

But . . . Giselle hadn't *left* campus with anyone. She hadn't left campus at all. Not . . . alive.

So . . . she must have said no when he came for her.

But in the letter, he said he wouldn't *take* no for an answer. Had he meant it? And if he had, what had he done or said in return for her *no* that was so awful it had driven Giselle to suicide?

Unless . . .

Jess sat up straight in bed. Her eyes stared blankly at the spot on the wall where, in her dream, the dreadful shadow had hung. Unless Giselle *hadn't* committed suicide.

The word "apparent" rang in her head. "Apparent suicide." "Apparent" meant that it *seemed* like suicide. But maybe it wasn't.

Jess awoke in the morning stiff and cramped, half-sitting, half-lying against the headboard. The weather outside was drizzly and gray, and cold, damp air drifted in through the open window.

She dressed quickly in jeans and the gray Salem U. sweatshirt, grateful for its fleecy warmth. Stuffing the photo and the letter in a rear jeans pocket, she hurried down to the kitchen. Everyone else was already eating breakfast.

The kitchen seemed dismal without the sun's warming rays streaming in through the wall of windows. The gray mist outside had made the rest of the world disappear, and the room became a dreary, isolated island.

Trucker had made coffee. Jess sipped the strong, hot liquid gratefully and took a seat at the table. Unhappy with the weather, her housemates barely grunted as she sat down. Only Ian smiled at her.

"I found something," Jess said when they were all seated. She placed the letter and the photo side by side on the wooden table between an open cereal box and a round tub of butter.

Cath lifted her head. "A dead body in the basement?" she said in a weary monotone. "It wouldn't surprise me."

Ian studied the picture. "Who is it, and who went crazy with the black marker?"

"I think it's Giselle McKendrick, and I'm sure the person who drew the slash mark is the same person who wrote the letter. I think the photo is some kind of threat."

The letter was passed around the table. "Well," Linda commented, "he's no poet, that's for sure. Doesn't have a way with words."

When the photo reached Milo, his face paled and the hand holding the picture trembled slightly.

"Is it her, Milo?" Jess asked gently.

He nodded, and swallowed hard. "Her hair looks longer, but it's her."

"There were other letters," Jess said, retrieving the picture and the letter. "He says so. They could be here somewhere."

"Then why did you only find *one*?" Cath asked.

"This one slid down behind the dresser."

When Trucker read the letter, his only comment was, "Tough guy. I know the type. All talk and no action."

Maybe, Jess thought. Maybe not. "I think I'm going to see if I can find those other letters."

"What's the point?" Ian said, sounding annoyed. "The girl is dead. Why do you want to play Sherlock Holmes?"

That rankled. Jess shot him a look of irritation. She had no intention of playing detective. She was just going to look for the letters.

It almost seemed as if he didn't *want* her finding any letters to Giselle. But why? What did Giselle have to do with Ian? They'd never even met.

Suddenly she remembered her conversation with the girl named Beth. She said she'd seen someone fighting with Giselle . . . someone tall, with long, dark hair.

Ian had been on campus last June. He'd said it was to check out the place.

But Jon had been on campus then, too. And hadn't he said he had a "thing" for blue-eyed blondes like Giselle?

And then there was Milo, who knew Giselle and hadn't told them. What if he'd never got over his feelings for Giselle?

He could have been fantasizing about her that whole time in high school, built that fantasy into a romance that never was. She'd read about people who did that. And you couldn't talk them out of it, no matter how hard you tried. Had Giselle suffered because of Milo's illusions?

"That poor girl," Cath said softly, glancing over Trucker's shoulder at the photograph. "So gorgeous . . . and so unhappy, taking her own life . . ."

The cellar door flew open and slammed violently against the wall.

Chapter 19

The slamming of the door stirred them all to action. While Trucker closed the cellar door and latched it, everyone else gathered together books and papers, windbreakers, and hooded sweatshirts against the weather, and straggled out of the house.

Between classes, Jess grabbed a sandwich in the student café with Linda. Conversation centered around the Fall Ball. It was a relief to forget about what was going on at the house and concentrate on something else.

"Milo hasn't asked me yet," Linda said gloomily. "I don't think he's going to. He's so darn *shy.*"

"Well, I can't quite see Milo in a tux," Jess remarked. She couldn't see Milo at a dance, either, for that matter. He seemed so antisocial.

"Oh, I can! He'd be gorgeous!"

Jess shrugged. "Maybe if he did something with that hair and that beard . . . like trimming them, for instance."

"I like his hair. I think he looks cool, artistic."

Artistic, Jess thought. Had Milo ever used a black marker in his artistic efforts? As in defacing a photograph? He had said that he and Giselle stopped being friends in high school. But he'd never said that was *okay* with him.

Maybe it hadn't been.

When Jess got home, Nightingale Hall looked even more forbidding than usual in the persistent fog and drizzle.

I don't really want to go in there, she thought, staring up at the dark brick structure.

But where else was there to go? She'd stalled on campus as long as possible, reading in the library. But she hadn't wanted to walk home alone after dark, so she had finally gathered her things together and walked, slowly, home.

Maybe everyone else would leave tonight and she could hunt for the rest of Giselle's letters. Where would they be, she wondered.

And that was when it occurred to Jess that maybe she wasn't the *only* person anxious to get her hands on those letters. Cath's missing paper, Linda's ruined bathing suit, the worms in her dresser drawer . . . what if . . . what if those were just smoke screens? What if they were just stupid pranks designed to cover up the fact that someone had actually been *hunting* for something in those rooms?

Something like . . . letters to a dead girl, letters that might be too revealing if they were discovered.

You are *so* melodramatic, she chided herself, shaking her head. You should have been an actress. The letters probably aren't even *here*.

But . . . maybe someone *thought* they were.

It couldn't hurt to look for them. If she found them, they might answer some of her questions about Giselle.

Ian was in the kitchen, alone. He helped her remove her soggy windbreaker and handed her a cup of steaming hot chocolate. "Nasty out there. How come you're late?"

"I was at the library. Research." She didn't add that she intended to do a different kind of research the minute she had an opportunity. He wouldn't understand her need to hunt for the letters.

They sat at the table, sipping silently in the dreary kitchen. Dozens of questions swirled around in Jess's mind, but she didn't share them with Ian. He'd think she was being silly.

Hadn't he said, "The girl is dead," and told her to forget about it?

But she couldn't do that. Jess wondered if Ian noticed the change in her mood toward him.

"So, did you toss that stuff?" he asked. He was wearing a thick white sweater, sleeves pushed to the elbows, and his high, angled cheekbones were wind-burnished, like hers. His dark eyes remained on her face as he said, "The picture and that letter? Did you dump them?"

"No. Not yet." Immediately, she regretted the admission. If someone *was* looking for the letters, maybe she should be pretending she'd tossed the one she'd found into the trash. And maybe . . . her stomach stirred uneasily . . . maybe she had made a mega-major mistake sharing the letter and photo at breakfast. If someone really *was* determined to find the missing letters, and *if* that person was one of her housemates . . . Who else would have access to their rooms . . . ? Maybe she should have kept her big mouth shut this morning.

Too late now.

"Jess, that's old news," Ian said, his voice unusually fierce. "What are you hanging onto that stuff for?"

"Actually," she said nonchalantly, "I think I left it somewhere on campus. So, I guess that's not really hanging on to it, right?"

"Oh. Well, good. There's something really morbid about carrying around a picture of a dead girl and one of her letters."

True. But then, there was something really morbid about the girl having died in the first place, wasn't there? Especially when there seemed to be some mystery about *why* she'd died.

The weather kept everyone inside, giving Jess no chance to hunt for the letters.

When Linda absolutely refused to stay in her room alone, saying staunchly, "There is safety in numbers," they all settled in the living room. Trucker built a generous fire in the stone fireplace, and the room quickly warmed.

Milo and Linda settled on the Persian rug near the blazing orange and yellow flames, while Jess and Cath plopped themselves down on the sofa and Trucker, Jon, and Ian occupied chairs scattered about the huge room.

The drizzle became a steady rain. Driven by the hilltop wind, it slapped against the windows. The room, with its smell of burning wood and the warmth from the fireplace, seemed a great place to be on such a night. Why can't it always be this nice, Jess thought.

She had barely finished thinking the question when Linda, becoming bored, stirred restlessly and asked Milo, "Why is your notebook so thick? You never finish anything, so what are all those papers in there?" Before he could answer, she made a playful grab for the blue spiral book and began leafing through it.

"Hand it over," he ordered lazily, reaching for the notebook.

Laughing, Linda held it high, beyond his reach.

Several papers slipped out and drifted to the floor. One landed at Cath's feet. She bent to pick it up.

And her eyes widened as they scanned the sheet. "I *knew* it!"

He looked up. "What?"

Cath stood up, staring at Milo, the sheet of paper still in her hands. "This is my essay. The one you said you didn't take!"

Everyone in the room stopped what they were doing to focus their attention on Cath, and on Milo, scrambling to his feet.

"It fell out of *your* notebook," she said, her eyes on his face. "You really *did* take it."

"No, I —"

"I was so sure at first." The ever-present lines of tension in Cath's face deepened. "But then, no one else thought so, and I decided maybe I was wrong. But . . . but here it *is*."

Jess's heart sank. Had Milo really stolen that essay, and lied about it?

The way he'd lied about knowing Giselle. Hadn't told the truth, anyway. The same thing, really.

"I *didn't* take your essay and I don't know how it got in my notebook," Milo said emphatically. "That's the truth. Believe it, don't believe it. Your choice." And bending to grab the blue notebook from a red-faced Linda's hands, he stalked from the room.

Aiming a disgusted look in Cath's direction, Linda got up and ran after him.

"Why did she look at *me* like that?" Cath said, glancing around the room. "*I* didn't do anything. It's not *my* fault my essay was in Milo's notebook." Near tears, she picked up her books and, head down, left the room.

It no longer seemed warm or cozy.

When Jon and Trucker had gone, Jess and Ian sat on the floor close to the fire's dying embers. "That *was* Cath's essay," she told him. "I saw it. It still had her name on it."

"I don't want to talk about that," he said firmly, taking her hands in his. "There's been too much crazy stuff going on around here, and it's getting to you, I can tell. I thought we had something going, but lately I'm not so sure." He took a deep breath and let it out. "I want you to go to that dance with me. That Fall Ball thing. I think that's what we need to do."

Jess smiled. "You make it sound like a prescription. Take one Fall Ball and call me in the morning."

"In a way, it is." He grinned. "Dr. Banion, at your service."

She wanted to say yes, of course she'd go to the ball with him. But — the person who had fought with Giselle on campus had long, dark hair. And Ian had acted so strangely since she'd found that letter to Giselle. Ian could have been Giselle's out-of-town boyfriend, couldn't he? And he could have been angry that she'd dumped him. And he could have put the worms in her drawer when he was hunting for the letters . . .

No!

"Come on, Jess," Ian urged softly. "Who needs a good time more than us?"

He hadn't lied about knowing Giselle. It was Milo who had done that, not Ian.

If she went to the dance would she be able to pretend, even for a few hours, that her life was as normal as any other Salem University student? Could she fool herself into thinking, in the brightly colored hall filled with music and laughter and dancing, that when it was all over, she'd be going home to a nice, safe, *normal* dorm?

Maybe. She could give it the old college try.

But . . . was Ian still the person she wanted to go to the dance with? Did she trust him?

She studied his face, bronzed by the flickering, dying flames. Anyone could be responsible for all the strange things that had happened at Nightingale Hall. *Anyone.* Anyone except Ian, she decided.

"Yes," she said, "I'd love to go to the ball with you."

Chapter 20

An opportunity to look for the rest of Giselle's letters came the following night, when everyone but Jess had left the house to attend a fraternity party.

"Not me," she announced after dinner. "I have a bad headache. I need a nice, long nap."

"You're going to stay here *alone*?" Linda asked, disbelief in her voice. "No, come with us."

"I can't," Jess said lightly, conscious of Ian's eyes on her. He looked disappointed, and she was afraid he'd offer to stay home with her.

He didn't. "Too bad about your headache," was all he said and, giving her a hug, he left with the others.

She was alone at last.

It made sense to begin her search in her own room, the one that had been Giselle's. Giselle might have tucked the letters away in a corner or shelf of the closet, if she hadn't thrown them away.

I would have, Jess thought as she braced herself against the chill in her room and pulled the door open. If the other letters were anything like the one I found, I'd have ripped them into tiny little fragments and fed them to the garbage disposal. No one has the right to threaten someone that way.

She found no letters in her room. Or any other evidence that Giselle McKendrick had once lived there.

Disappointed, she was about to make her way down the hall to Linda's room and try there, when she heard a noise from downstairs.

They couldn't be home already. She hadn't been searching for more than half an hour.

A flicker of light from outside drew her to the window. A pale yellow circle moved near the in-ground cellar doors. Trucker? Hadn't he gone to the party, too? Ian had planned to invite him. Jon, who was driving everyone, had laughed and said, "You guys are going to be piled on top of each other in my Beemer." But he hadn't said Trucker wasn't welcome to join them.

Maybe Trucker hadn't felt like going.

Just then, her overhead light went out.

Reaching behind her for the desk lamp, Jess pushed on its switch.

Nothing happened.

She tried again. But her room remained black as night. The bulb must have burned out.

Jess, a small voice somewhere in her head murmured, what are the chances that the bulbs in your overhead light *and* your desk lamp would die at exactly the same moment?

She was *not* going to get upset. Maybe Trucker was working in the cellar and had to turn off the electricity for some reason. He could be working on the furnace. He had said he needed to check it out before cold weather hit.

But . . . hadn't he said it was a gas furnace? Why would he need to turn off the electricity?

Maybe he was working on something else, something electrical. He probably didn't even know anyone was home. Probably thought she had gone to the party with the others.

Feeling her way in the dark, Jess made her way across the room to the door and opened it. The hall was pitch-dark. She felt for the wall switch, flipped it several times, but nothing happened.

The electricity was definitely off at Nightingale Hall.

It seemed to take her forever to wend her way downstairs and into the kitchen. When she reached the cellar door, she hesitated.

What if it wasn't Trucker down there? What if he'd gone to the party when Ian invited him, and someone *else*, thinking the house empty, was in the cellar . . . maybe hunting for something? Hunting for, say, some incriminating letters?

No sound echoed up from the cellar. Maybe there wasn't *anyone* down there now. If the light she'd seen had belonged to Trucker, he could have finished what he was working on and gone back to his apartment over the garage.

But then . . . the electricity would be back on and . . . she flicked the switch beside the door . . . it wasn't.

There was only one way to find out. She had absolutely no intention of going down into that damp, musty cellar. But she had to know if Trucker was down there, in which case she would ask him to turn the electricity back on.

And if Trucker *wasn't* down there, she'd go over to his apartment to remind him about the electricity.

It wasn't like him to forget something like that.

She unlatched the cellar door and pulled it open. "Trucker?" she called softly.

Not a glimmer of light shone upward. Trucker wouldn't be down there without a light. He'd have a lantern or flashlight with him.

He wasn't down there. She'd have to go find him and tell him about the electricity.

She moved to slam the door shut and latch it.

Too late. A blow between her shoulder blades stole her breath and knocked her off-balance. She teetered precariously at the edge of the cellar stairs, her hands reaching out for something, anything . . .

And then a second, more forceful blow sent her off her feet and out into the black void, flying out and down, down, down . . .

She couldn't catch her breath to scream.

She landed at the foot of the staircase, her head striking the hard, earthen floor with a sharp crack.

In that last, final second before she lost consciousness, she heard the door at the top of the stairs slam shut and the metal latch click into place.

Chapter 21

Jess came back to awareness slowly, painfully. She could see nothing. Her left elbow throbbed. Her head hurt. And she had no idea where she was.

Trying to remember was like pushing her way through a thick, cottony fog. What was she doing in this cold, damp, dark place that smelled of earth and mold and . . . something else . . . something sweetish?

A sinister hissing sound off to her left brought her head up, snapped her eyes completely open. That sweet, sickening smell, the hissing . . . the smell was gas, the hiss a leak. Gas was leaking from somewhere near her.

She remembered then. She had been shoved down the cellar stairs, had hit her head, been knocked out.

She was in the cellar and there was a gas leak.

It took her long, agonizing moments to force herself to a sitting position and then, reaching backward to grip the stair railing for support, pull herself completely upright. If only it weren't so dark . . .

Shaky and dazed, she was clear-minded enough to know she had to get out of the cellar, which was rapidly filling with gas.

The door at the top of the stairs was locked, she remembered. She had heard the latch slide into place. Someone had shoved her down here and didn't want her to leave.

Why *not*? she screamed silently.

But there was another way out. The outside cellar doors, the ones Trucker used. Where *were* they? Jess peered into the darkness. Which direction? Where was the front of the house?

She struggled to form a diagram in her mind, using the kitchen above her as a guideline. It worked. There, in *that* direction, straight ahead. The cellar doors should be *there*.

She staggered, one hand to her aching elbow, the other hand protecting her mouth and nose from the gas, through a maze of boxes and cartons and trunks, until her sneakered foot bumped against the bottom stone step that led the way up and out through the wooden doors.

Silently rejoicing, she lifted her arms and pushed upward with all of her strength, tears of pain spilling down her cheeks as her injured elbow screamed a protest.

But her efforts were in vain. The heavy wooden doors never moved. The rattling sound she heard was probably the padlock, securely fastened on the outside.

Jess sagged against the stone wall. No way out . . . And the hissing continued.

I don't want to die in here, she thought clearly, her eyes searching through the darkness for help. I have to stop that gas . . .

It had to be coming from the furnace. Trucker called it the heater from hell, saying it was a huge old thing from the Dark Ages. If it was that big, it shouldn't be hard to find even in the dark.

I don't *want* to do this, she thought, fighting tears. I want *out* of here!

Biting her lip and swiping at the tears, she told herself angrily, quit whining. Find that gas line!

Gingerly moving forward, Jess took tiny steps, making little circles in the air with first one foot, then the other. Twice, a sneaker came into contact with something, but both times the object was small and soft: a pile of rags, a bundle of old clothing?

She kept going. Her senses alert, she followed the hissing sound until she bumped up against the huge, unmoving pile of metal in the middle of the room . . . the furnace.

Her headache was growing worse every second, hammering away at her skull. Using her injured arm, she crooked it at the elbow and scooped the bottom of her sweatshirt up against her mouth and nose. Listening carefully, she located the source of the ominous hissing. It was coming from directly below where she stood. She crouched, exploring with her hand. The hand found a cold metal pipe at the base of the furnace. The hissing came from there.

All she had to do now was find the valve, turn it, and the hissing . . . the gas flow . . . would stop.

Her fingers moved to the end of the pipe, where the valve would be.

There . . . was . . . no . . . valve.

Someone had removed it.

Someone had made it impossible for her to stop the flow of gas.

Jess sank back on her haunches, moaning, "Oh, no . . ."

A fit of coughing seized her. She grasped the sides of the boiler to pull herself up and her right hand touched something soft . . .

There was something caught on a nail above her head, something that felt like old wool. She could use it to cover her mouth and nose.

She tugged, gently at first, then more forcefully. The scrap of soft cloth came off the nail with a tearing sound. She put it over her mouth and nose, pressing it close to her skin.

It helped. But she still had to find a way to stop the gas flow.

Kneeling, she walked on her knees all the way around the metal structure. There *had* to be a way.

The floor was cold and rough. Through her jeans, she could feel the skin scraping from her knees. There *had* to be something . . .

She found nothing on the furnace. But when she gave up her search and sagged back against the wall, something poked her shoulder. She turned around, felt with her fingers. A small, cold, metal wheel with little spokes in the center. It jutted out from the wall and when she followed it with her fingers, it led directly to the furnace.

It was worth a try.

She placed her hand on the small wheel and turned.

But it didn't move.

She would have to use both hands, no matter how much the effort hurt her elbow.

Gritting her teeth, she tried again. And was rewarded with the tiniest of movements and a loud creaking sound. Again, and again, and again, she threw her weight behind her turning motion, groaning aloud with the terrible pain in her left arm.

"I *am* going to do this, do you hear me?" she shouted. "I *am!*"

Slowly, so slowly, the creaky old valve moved in a gradual circle until she could turn it no more.

The hissing stopped.

Jess sank back on her heels again, sobbing gratefully.

But the air in the cellar was still poisonous. She had to get out of there.

It was then that she saw the window. High up on the front wall. The glass was so filthy it was gray, and blended into the wall as if it were just another block of stone.

It was small, and very high up.

Coughing spasmodically, her left arm and her head throbbing, Jess used her feet to push a heavy trunk into place directly underneath the window. With that in place, she stuffed the woolen square into a back pocket of her jeans. Her hand free, she yanked an old wooden chair onto the top of the trunk.

She was breathing hard from her efforts, but her "ladder" was in place.

Carefully, slowly, she climbed onto the trunk and then onto the chair seat, balancing gingerly as she stood up straight and found her chest even with the windowsill.

She heaved a sigh of relief.

And, a minute later, began weeping with rage because the window wouldn't open. The latch, like the valve, was old and rusted and petrified within its little metal hook.

There was only one way she was going to get out through this little window. Smashing glass was dangerous. Hadn't they nearly been sliced to ribbons by the exploding mirror in Linda's room? But being on the outside with a few scratches would be better than remaining in this dark, clammy hole unscratched.

Reaching down and backward, she pulled off one of her sneakers to use as a hammer. It took several blows of increasing strength to shatter the first pane. Fresh air flowed in, and Jess gulped it in gratefully.

She made short work of the remaining three panes. As she slammed away with the shoe, she was vaguely aware of stinging sensations on her hands, neck, and face, but she ignored them. She would worry about any damage done later, when she was free.

With the glass gone, it took her only a few more minutes to destroy the old, rotting wood that had held the panes in place.

Then she put her shoe back on and hoisted her body through the small opening, praying she wouldn't get stuck on her way out. She cried out in pain when her injured elbow slammed against the stone wall, but she kept going, hauling her legs up behind her and thrusting her body out over the sill onto the ground.

She was free. Her head ached, her arm burned with pain, and her stomach heaved with nausea, but she was *free*.

Gasping in cool, fresh air, she lay limply on her stomach, too exhausted, for the moment, to push herself upright. She closed her eyes in relief.

When she opened them a moment later, the first thing she saw was a pair of dirty white sneakers with orange laces.

Someone was standing over her.

Chapter 22

Jess waited for a cry of, "Why, Jess, what are you doing down there?" And a gentle hand to help her up.

But no cry of sympathy came, no hand reached down to help her. The only sound breaking through the cool darkness was her own ragged breathing.

Then a voice from above whispered, "Oh, please, don't get up on my account." And a sneakered foot came down on her back, pinioning her to the ground.

Her blood froze.

He'd been waiting for her.

"Think you're pretty smart, don't you?" the voice hissed. "Getting out of the cellar . . . you weren't supposed to *do* that, Jess."

He knew her name. And there was something about the voice . . . But it was only a whisper. She couldn't identify a whisper.

"Couldn't leave well enough alone, could you? You were the *only* one who caught on . . . Giselle's death had already been forgotten. But you guessed the truth when you read that letter you found, didn't you?"

If she could just lift herself up, she would be able to see who it was. But with his foot pinning her down, she was helpless. Not being able to see him when he was so very close was maddening. And terrifying.

"I knew you were lying when you said you had a headache. You were going to look for those letters, that's why you wanted to be alone. Busybody!" The whisper deepened. "You *lied*, like Giselle lied. She said she would marry me, but she only said that to humor me. So I'd let her go off to college. She said it was just for one year. Then we'd get married, she said." The whisper spat fury at Jess. "But she *lied*! I knew it when she didn't answer my letters or phone calls."

And Jess knew then that he was going to kill her. She was going to die right here on the ground in front of Nightingale Hall, behind the wall of shrubbery. Her body might not be found for days.

"I . . . I didn't *find* the letters," she stammered.

A whispered laugh. "Well, *I* know that! *I* found them. In the trunk. And I hid them. But you guessed the truth. I can't have that. I really can't."

Jess's arms were free, outstretched on either side of her. Her hands explored the darkness, fumbled . . . there had to be something . . . a rock, a stick, some weapon . . .

Her left hand encountered something sharp . . . a shard of glass from the broken cellar window. It was thick, and the sides were razor-sharp. When her fingers curled around it, the edges dug into the skin of her palm. But it was all she had, and she bit her lip to keep from crying out in pain.

And then he was on her, straddling her back, and something thick and rough was encircling her throat. A rope, digging into her skin. It hurt.

She knew she had only seconds. He was going to tighten the rope, cut off her air, strangle her.

Just as he'd strangled Giselle.

Jess's hand tightened on the piece of glass. Sticky warmth flowed from her palm. But she held on.

He was leaning forward over her, his mouth close to her ear. "Take your last breath, Jess.

It will feel delicious. The last one always does. Just ask Giselle . . ."

The noose tightened, shutting off her air supply. She was still feeling weak and sick from the gas in the cellar, and her head began to swim.

In one desperate, swift movement, she brought her left arm up and backward, slashing wildly with the piece of glass.

Her attacker shouted an oath. The rope around her neck eased its grip.

And then the driveway was illuminated by a bright yellow light, and there was the crunching sound of tires on gravel.

The weight left her back, taking the cruel rope with it. "Damn!" came an angry whisper. "You'll be sorry for this! You'll pay!" And the sneakers turned and ran.

Jess tried to lift her head. A car? Jon's BMW? Her friends were home. She wouldn't be alone now. *He* wouldn't come back now, because he couldn't deal with all of them.

But it wasn't them. The yellow glow faded as the car backed out of the driveway. It had only been turning around.

If *he* saw that, would he come back? Or was he long gone? She should get up, should run, run . . . but she was so dizzy . . .

I'm still alive, Jess thought, dazed. I didn't die, like Giselle.

But . . . he wasn't "finished" with her.

She tried to get up. She had only made it to her knees when a wave of dizziness slammed her back to the ground, eyes closing as she fell, unconscious.

Chapter 23

Jess was jolted back to consciousness by the slamming of car doors, followed by laughter, as Jon's BMW arrived home and everyone jumped out and began to run to the house through the light rain.

She heard Ian say, "Hey, Jess didn't leave any lights on for us. Can't see my nose in front of my face. Trucker, go hit the lights, will you?"

Jess's voice was so weak, she had to call out four times before they heard her. Several more minutes passed before they located her behind the wall of bushes.

Jess immediately began babbling her story. But no one could make any sense of it. When the lights came on, they helped her into the house. Seated on a chair in the hall, she calmed down enough to tell her story, although her voice shook. "He . . . he said he wasn't finished with me," she concluded, shivering with fear and cold.

"How long have you been lying out there?" Ian asked. "Your clothes are soaked, and you're freezing." He took off his windbreaker and wrapped it around her.

"I don't know. A long time, I guess. I was so afraid he'd come back, I tried to get up. But I must have fainted."

It was Cath who asked, "Did you see who it was, Jess?"

"No. But he had orange laces in his shoes. The glow-in-the-dark kind."

"Well, *that's* no clue," Jon said. And Jess knew he was right. They sold those by the thousands at the bookstore. It was a cheap way to promote the school's colors. Everyone wore them.

As one, they glanced down. Everyone except Cath, in black ballet slippers, had orange-laced sneakers.

Trucker returned, reporting, "It was the master switch. Someone flipped it off. Why would someone do that?"

Ian sensed that Jess wouldn't want to repeat her story, and filled Trucker in on why someone had *done* that.

Trucker's thick, dark brows furrowed together in a scowl. "Man, I don't *believe* this! A gas leak? Jess, you okay?"

She nodded, but that hurt her head, so she stopped.

"You never should have stayed here alone," Linda scolded, but she patted Jess's shoulder at the same time. "But . . . but I never thought someone would try to . . . *kill* you!"

"You didn't see anything?" Ian asked. "Maybe we should search the cellar, see if he left any clues."

Jess lifted her head. "There *was* something." Grimacing in pain, she reached into her back jeans pocket for the swatch of fabric she had held over her mouth and nose in the cellar. "This was hanging on a nail above the furnace."

The small square was maroon. The fabric was soft, worn, and heavy.

"Like a baseball jacket," she mused aloud, fingering the material. "I've . . . I've seen a jacket like this . . . somewhere . . ." Then, "I remember. It was in Milo's room. That day we — " She glanced around. "Where *is* Milo? Didn't he come home with you?"

"He didn't *go* with us," Jon said. "Changed his mind. Said he had something he had to do."

Jess regarded him with thoughtful eyes. "Milo didn't go to the party with you? He was . . . he was *here*?"

"Well, of course he wasn't *here*," Linda said crossly. "He'd have *helped* you if he were here. He said he had to go somewhere."

Jess sat quietly, lost in thought, shivering in Ian's windbreaker. When she spoke again, it was to ask Trucker, "When you were in the cellar getting that trunk for Avery Mc-Kendrick, why did you come upstairs?"

"Milo wanted a soda."

"Milo sent you upstairs?" Jess clamped her lips together. "So he could be alone with the trunk?"

"Jess!" Linda cried. "What are you thinking?"

Jess stood up. "I'm going upstairs now," she said distinctly, "And I'm going to search Milo's room. Anyone who wants to, can help me. But," directing a level gaze at Linda, "*no* one is going to stop me."

"You need dry clothes," Cath said. "You're soaked and you're shivering."

"Later."

They all followed her up the stairs. She stopped at her room to collect the one letter she'd found, stuffing it into a pocket of her jeans. Then they moved on to Milo's room, where everyone but Linda, who remained stubbornly in the doorway, arms folded over her chest, helped Jess search Milo's room for the missing letters.

It was Jess who found them. They were paper-clipped together, without envelopes, in a bottom dresser drawer under a jumble of T-shirts.

"You can stop looking for the letters," she announced, taking the sheets of paper to the unmade bed and sitting on it. "I found them."

Everyone fell silent as Jess began reading.

Hey, Babe,
How come I haven't heard from you? No letters, no phone calls. When I call there, they say you're not home. You shouldn't be out so much. You're supposed to be studying. They wouldn't be lying to me, would they? You wouldn't be telling them to, would you? You'd better call me.

It was signed only, *Your Forever Love.*
The second letter was angrier:

Giselle,
If I don't hear from you soon, I'm coming
out there. We had a bargain. You had to
have one year of college, you said. Then
you'd marry me, that's what you said.
Now, I think you were lying. I think you
just said that to get away from me. You
shouldn't have done that. If that's what
you did, you'll be sorry.

Your Forever Love

Linda moved into the room, her eyes wide
with apprehension.

Jess read the third letter:

Giselle,
I've been patient. I've given you plenty
of time to call me. Now my patience
is gone. Did you really think I'd just let
you go? I can't do that. You're my for-
ever love, remember? If you met some rich
college guy, you can forget about him.
You belong to me. Forever. You have one
more chance to call me and tell me you're
coming with me in June. Don't fail me,

Giselle. I don't want to have to punish you.

Your Forever Love

"He doesn't *sound* very loving," Cath commented.

"The letter I found in my room," Jess said, pulling it from her pocket, "has to be the last one. It's the angriest one."

Giselle,
Your time has run out. I'm coming to get you and you'd better be ready to come with me. I'm not taking no for an answer.

Your Forever Love

Jess dropped the letter and lifted her head. "And I think that 'no' is the answer that Giselle *gave* him. But I don't think he accepted it."

"What are you talking about?" Linda asked. Her face was bone-white.

She knows what I'm going to say, Jess thought. Poor Linda. "I don't think Giselle McKendrick committed suicide. I think the person who wrote these letters killed her and made it *look* like suicide."

"Well, it wasn't Milo!" Linda cried, backing away from Jess.

"Linda." Jess began ticking items off on her fingers. "He lied about knowing Giselle. He volunteered to go into the cellar to help Trucker with her trunk, and then sent Trucker upstairs so he could look through the trunk for the letters. Don't you get it, Linda? The letters are what Milo was looking for in *our* rooms. We thought it was vandalism, but it wasn't. He was searching for the letters."

Linda chewed on her lower lip.

"Milo was afraid someone else would find the letters," Jess continued. "These threatening letters would make people suspicious about Giselle's death. And Milo finally did find the letters, in the trunk. But there was still the one *I'd* found."

Linda frowned. "That trunk was in the cellar a long time. Anyone could have taken those letters."

"Linda, Milo was the only one who wasn't at the party when I was attacked. And I know it was someone from Nightingale Hall, because he said he knew I'd lied when I said I had a headache."

"Oh, everyone was running in and out of that party all night long," Linda said angrily. "Ian left for a while, and so did Jon. *They* could have come back here." Her voice rose. "It *wasn't* Milo!"

"What wasn't Milo?" a voice said from the doorway.

All heads turned to face Milo. He was leaning against the door. And he was wearing a wool, maroon baseball jacket. A large, three-cornered tear was clearly visible on the left shoulder.

Chapter 24

"Why are you guys holding a convention in my room?" Milo asked, advancing into the room. His thin face was flushed, his eyes angry behind his glasses.

Jess left the bed and went to stand against the wall between Cath and Trucker. "Your jacket is torn, Milo. How did that happen? As if I didn't know."

Milo shrugged. "Then *you* tell *me*. I haven't been able to find this jacket for a couple of weeks. Tonight, I was working downstairs at the library and when I went back upstairs to get my books, the jacket was there, hanging on my chair. With a *rip* in it. Weird."

"Yeah, weird," Trucker said cynically.

"Milo," Linda said hesitantly, "I was at the library tonight, just for a minute. I dropped off some books on my way to the theater. I . . . . I didn't see you there."

Another shrug. "I was there. All night."

"*You?*" Jess's laugh was harsh. "At the library? Oh, right. We *know* where you were, Milo. You were here, sabotaging the furnace and pushing me down the cellar stairs and . . ."

"What is she talking about?" Milo directed his question toward Ian.

"She thinks you *killed* Giselle!" Linda burst out, "and than you tried to kill *her* . . . Jess . . . tonight. I *told* her you didn't, but she found a piece of material on a nail in the cellar where the gas leak was, and it's the same as your jacket and now you have that rip . . ." Linda began crying quietly.

"And so now you agree with Jess," Milo told Linda softly. "Because of a rip in my jacket that I didn't put there."

"And because of the letters," Cath added. "To Giselle. We found them here, in your room. You got them out of Giselle's trunk and hid them."

"I never wrote Giselle any letters. I told you, we weren't friends anymore."

"Well, *that's* for sure," Jess cried. "I certainly wouldn't call these letters friendly. They're full of threats, which is why you had to find them . . . before someone else did and guessed what really happened to Giselle."

"Is my name on those letters?"

"Well . . . no. They're signed 'Your Forever Love.' But we know you wrote them."

Milo laughed bitterly. "You think I was Giselle McKendrick's 'forever love'? I wasn't even her forever *friend*."

"And that made you really angry, didn't it, Milo?" Jess said. "Angry enough to kill her . . ."

And then there was a long, long moment of painful silence. Milo stood with his hands at his sides, looking from one face to the next, something in his eyes . . .

He's angry, Jess thought, watching him. He's furious that we found him out. He thought he'd covered his tracks so well.

Then Milo said, his voice devoid of emotion, "You all agree with Jess?"

No one said they didn't.

He turned and headed for the closet. Silently, he began stuffing clothes into a blue duffel bag.

"What are you doing?" Jess took a step toward the closet.

The bag full, Milo turned again. "I'm leaving."

Jess stared at him. "Leave? You can't leave!"

"Why not? Did you call the police?"

"No, I . . ."

"And you won't. You can't. You have no proof, nothing to show them. My name isn't on those letters. There are thousands of these jackets. And anyone could have taken those letters from the trunk and put them in my drawer. You've got nothing, Jess."

"Ian?" Jess appealed. But he shrugged. "He's right, Jess. We don't have anything concrete."

"We can't just let him walk out of here. He killed that girl and he tried to kill *me*!"

"Well, until you can prove that cockamamie story," Milo said, "I'm out of here. I'll pick up the rest of my stuff later. Don't anyone touch my stuff, or you'll be sorry."

"That's what you told Giselle in one of the letters," Jess said, tears of frustration beginning to pool in her eyes. "You said she'd be sorry. And I'm sure she was . . . sorry that she ever *met* you."

Milo turned on his heel and was gone. They heard his soft footsteps padding down the hall, down the stairs . . . and then the front door slammed.

Jess ran to the open window and shouted at

him, "You won't get away with this, Milo! We'll *find* proof and you'll be punished!" Then, exhausted and frustrated, she began to sob.

Ian was at her side, wrapping her in his arms, soothing her. "It's okay, it's okay. We'll find something . . . there's time. He won't go far, not right away. His things are still here."

"Right," Cath agreed. "He'd never leave his precious notebooks here. He'll be back. Maybe we'll find something . . ."

Jess *did* find something, one week later, the day of the Fall Ball. It took her that long to steel herself to go into Milo's room and pack up his things. She wanted to come back after the ball to a house free of any traces of Milo Keith. With Mrs. Coates still hospitalized, Jess had to do it. Trucker and, to Jess's surprise, Linda, offered to help.

Jess found the typewriter on the floor of Milo's closet, under a pile of discarded clothing. "There's a typewriter in here!" she called out when she had unearthed the old machine. "An ancient one. I never heard Milo using a typewriter."

"That's because he didn't know how," Linda said. "The few papers he actually finished were scrawled in those awful hieroglyphics of his. I don't know how anyone could even read them."

"But the *letters* were typed," Jess pointed out. She picked up the paper-clipped letters. "I . . . I want to try something. Hand me a clean sheet of paper."

She inserted the blank paper into the old machine and began typing away furiously, copying the first two paragraphs of one of Giselle's letters. That done, she yanked the paper free.

"There," she declared triumphantly, "see?" She pointed. "See the 'O'? It's all filled in with ink. The 'O' is the same on Giselle's letters and on the paper I just typed in this machine. And look at the 'G' in Giselle. It's broken. It looks like a 'C'. *This* is the machine that typed those letters to Giselle, and this machine was in Milo's closet." She locked Linda's eyes with her own. "He lied to you about not being able to type. *Now* do you believe we were right about him?"

One of the saddest things Jess had ever seen was the look on Linda's face when the truth sank in. She looked like an abandoned child. "He never really cared about me, anyway," she said quietly. "I tried to pretend he did, but he didn't."

"You wouldn't really want him to, would you? I mean, he 'cared' about Giselle, and look what happened to her."

Linda nodded miserably, and hurried out of the room.

Jess was disappointed that Ian didn't jump at the chance to take the typewriter and the letters to the police. "All we've got," he said when she went to him, "is proof that this typewriter was used in those threatening letters to Giselle. But we *can't* prove that it's Milo's machine or that he typed the letters."

She knew he was right. But it was so *wrong* for Milo to get off scot-free.

"Look," Ian said, seeing her disappointment, "on Monday, we'll take the typewriter and the letters and anything else we have and go talk to someone at the police station. Maybe they'll laugh at us. But it's worth a try. But tonight," he added firmly, "we've got a dance to go to. And I don't want to hear the names Milo Keith or Giselle McKendrick mentioned, okay?"

Knowing that they were going to take action on Monday cleared the way for Jess to relax and get ready for the dance.

The three girls got dressed in Cath's room.

Jess had borrowed a very simple black velvet dress from a classmate. Cath's dress was like a pale blue cloud. Linda, fighting hard to be cheerful, wore a very short, pretty dress of pale pink.

"I just wish I were going with someone I was crazy about," Cath moaned. She had piled her hair on top of her head, with little dark ringlets clustered around her ears. "All this effort, just for boring old Peter Oakes. Seems kind of wasted."

"Don't be negative," Jess scolded. "You never know who you might meet there. Someone could see you from across a crowded room and, like the song says, fall madly in love with you."

"You mean like you and Ian. Don't I wish?" Cath grimaced into her mirror, showing perfect small, white teeth. "I don't have time to be in love, anyway. It's not on my parents' schedule."

Jess laughed. "Cath, I don't think your parents are half as bad as you make them sound. I think *you're* the one who drives you crazy, not them."

Cath laughed, too. "You could be right. I can't seem to shake twelve years of goal-orienting, that's all."

It was wonderful to hear her laugh. Jess couldn't remember the last time she'd heard Cath laugh like that.

There was a lot of laughter that night. The huge room had been transformed, softly lit with theater lights of scarlet and orange and rust and violet hidden behind floor-to-ceiling panels of pale, wispy gauze, giving the entire room a dreamy, romantic quality. The music was alternately fast, hot, and upbeat, then slow and sweet.

Jess and Ian moved together as if they had always danced with each other, their bodies completely in tune.

Cath surprised them by dancing by, more than once, in the arms of Jon, who grinned at them triumphantly.

"Poor Peter," Jess murmured even as she returned Jon's grin.

"Who's Peter?" Ian asked.

"Nobody."

Trucker came to the dance stag. Cath let out a soft, "Wow," when she saw him standing in the doorway, and Linda said, "I just realized who Trucker looks like. Tom Selleck, only shorter. Every girl in this place is staring at him."

It was true.

Jess danced with him twice. He was a very

good dancer. "Is there anything you don't know how to do?" she asked him.

Trucker grinned. "Yep. Get rich."

She danced the last dance with Ian. This is the way it should have been since school started, she thought, smiling into Ian's chest. If it hadn't been for Milo . . .

She shivered involuntarily. Ian tightened his arms around her. "You okay?" he asked into her hair.

"Oh, yes," she murmured, "I am definitely okay."

The sweet, lovely hours had raced by and suddenly it was time to go home.

And for the first time in a long time, the thought of returning to Nightingale Hall didn't make Jess sick with anxiety.

Chapter 25

After the dance, Jess and Ian decided against "going for eats," as Jon put it. They weren't hungry. And a leisurely walk home on a clear, moonlit night seemed like a perfect opportunity for some time alone.

When they reached Nightingale Hall, it seemed to Jess, for the first time, welcoming. They had left the parlor and library lights blazing, and a nearly full moon overhead bathed the hill in a soft, silvery glow. The wind had gone to sleep, allowing the oak branches overhead to form a peaceful, protective canopy. Nothing about the place seemed frightening.

If I could paint, Jess thought as they made their way up the hill, I would paint what I'm looking at now. I'd make it all silver and black and gold and I'd make it romantic, like this night.

"Feel like sitting outside for a while?" Ian

asked. "Till the rest of the crew gets home?"

"Great idea, but I'll have to run in and get a jacket. It's cold out here."

"I'll get it. Tell me where."

Jess sat down on the top porch step. "In my room, on the floor. The blue denim jacket." She grinned. "It'll look *smashing* with this black velvet dress and heels."

"Gotcha! Be right back." Ian turned and hurried into the house. She could hear his footsteps thudding up the stairs.

Jess sighed happily. They would have precious moments alone until the others got back. What a great way to end a great night!

Maybe their housemates would eat and eat and they'd all be gone for hours.

A car pulled up in front of the house. A girl jumped out and began hurrying up the driveway.

Jess stood up. It wasn't Cath or Linda or anyone else she knew. Jess moved down the steps to greet the girl. Maybe she was looking for directions.

"Hi!" the small, dark-haired girl said as she arrived, breathless, at the top of the hill. "Is Milo home?"

Jess drew in her breath. "Milo?"

The girl handed Jess a blue windbreaker.

"I'm Daisy Lindgren. Milo and I were studying at the library last week. It rained and I didn't have a jacket, so he loaned me this windbreaker." She laughed. "It was weird . . . we left our stuff upstairs to work down in the computer room and when we came back up, there was another jacket on Milo's chair. He said it was his, but he'd lost it. Had no idea how it got there. And boy, was he ticked off when he saw a big tear on one shoulder. Said it hadn't been there before. Anyway, since he had *two* jackets and I didn't have any, he loaned me this windbreaker. Could you see that he gets it, please?"

Jess took the windbreaker. A sudden sense of dread came over her. Milo had said he was at the library that terrible Friday night. And he had said his jacket was missing. "When . . . when were you at the library with Milo?" she asked, her voice sounding hoarse and ragged. "What night last week exactly?" Don't say Friday, she prayed, do not say Friday.

"When?" Daisy Lindgren frowned. "Well, let's see, I had chorus practice on Wednesday, and I went shopping for shoes on Thursday, so it was . . . Friday. I was at the library with Milo on Friday night."

Chapter 26

"How long were you in the library with Milo?" Jess asked, forcing the words out. The girl would say she had been with Milo only for a few minutes Friday evening. Maybe half an hour. After that, Jess told herself, he came back to Nightingale Hall to sabotage the furnace valve, push me down the cellar stairs, and wait for me outside the window. Because that *is* what Milo did.

"How long? All night. We got there about eight, I think, and stayed until midnight, when the library closed." The pretty face screwed up into a frown. "Why?

"You couldn't have been there all that time," Jess said desperately, wishing Ian would return. "Linda — my housemate — was there. If Milo had been there, Linda would have seen him."

"We were downstairs. At the computers."

Jess's stomach was doing somersaults. Milo had been downstairs at the library last Friday night for four hours? No . . .

"Our world history professor told Milo he wouldn't accept one more handwritten paper from Milo. Said he couldn't read his hen-scratching. Milo can't type and he doesn't have a typewriter. I couldn't read his handwriting, either, so he had to dictate his paper to me while I typed it into the computer."

Milo didn't have a typewriter? He couldn't type? Of course he could. He had typed those letters to Giselle . . .

Hadn't he?

There was a pause as Jess struggled for the right questions to ask, questions that would give her the answers she wanted to hear.

"*Where* is Milo?" the girl asked again.

"He's . . . he's not here." There weren't any "right" questions. She had already asked the questions, and Daisy had given her the answers. And Daisy had told the truth, Jess was sure of that. Sickeningly sure.

Why hadn't Milo told them he couldn't type? Why hadn't he said he couldn't have written the letters because he couldn't type? Why hadn't he *told* them he wasn't alone at the library, that a girl from school could provide an ironclad alibi for him?

Jess knew the answer. Because no one would have believed him. They had already made up their minds.

"Thanks for bringing Milo's jacket," Jess told the girl. Her whole body felt numb. "I'll see that he gets it."

But, of course, she couldn't do that. She had no idea where Milo had gone.

His thin, bearded face danced before her eyes. And she realized then that what she had seen in his face that Friday night hadn't been anger, after all. It had been pain. Simple pain. Because the people he lived with had judged and convicted him unjustly.

A car horn sounded at the bottom of the hill.

"Gotta go," Daisy said. "Listen, tell Milo I'm sorry I didn't get the jacket to him sooner, okay?" She gave Jess a quizzical look. "You never did say where Milo is, exactly. Oh, well, see you."

As she turned and ran down the hill, the short, full skirt of her dress whipping out behind her, Jess thought, I want to go with her. I want to run down the hill, too, and up the road for miles and miles until I'm so far away from here that I will be able to forget Nightingale Hall and what we did to Milo Keith.

But she knew there was no place far enough away for that.

"Jess!"

A voice, calling her name. It sounded like it was coming from behind the house.

It came again, her name shouted with urgency. And it *was* coming from behind the house. It had to be Ian calling her. No one else was home. She hadn't seen him come outside, but he could have taken the fire escape. What was he doing out back?

Shivering with cold, Jess turned and hurried around the side of the house. There was no one there.

"Ian?" she called. "Where *are* you?"

"Jess, I'm down here!" The voice was coming now from the creek that meandered through the woods at the bottom of the slope behind the house. Through the trees, she could see a faint golden glow on the rushing water. Ian must have a flashlight. What on *earth* was he doing in the woods?

Jess smiled. Maybe Ian thought a creek in the woods was a really romantic spot.

"Hurry *up*!" he called. "You've got to see this!"

She'd have to remove her shoes. Trying to climb down the slope in high heels would be insane.

Carrying the shoes in one hand, she aimed for the yellow glow, pushing aside a final clump of undergrowth as she arrived at the creek.

"Ian," she began over the babble of the rushing creek, and then stopped as her eyes were automatically drawn to a spot illuminated in the water by the broad beam of the flashlight. There was something there, submerged. A large piece of paper . . . its top edges firmly pinioned by a smooth, gray rock, its bottom edges flapping frantically as the rapidly moving water pulled and tugged at it.

Her curiosity aroused, Jess bent to peer more closely into the creek. It wasn't a piece of paper. It was a . . . photograph. Of a girl. A beautiful girl. Even with the eerie distortion caused by the flowing water, turned a garish yellow by the flashlight's glow, Jess could clearly make out the features.

The girl in the watery photograph was Giselle McKendrick.

And the photograph fluttering in the creek had been defaced with the same ugly black slash mark that marred the smaller photo found by Jess in her room.

Jess gasped and turned to face Ian.

But it wasn't Ian, after all, aiming the flashlight at the photograph. It was Trucker.

"I didn't know you were home," Jess said, frowning. "Where's Ian?"

"I left the dance early." Trucker shrugged. "No one noticed. Came home, changed my clothes, and decided to fish for a while." He was wearing a plaid flannel shirt, open at the throat, and jeans. "Milo put this picture here, Jess. A few minutes ago. I saw him, but he didn't see me. He put it there, then he called you, and ran. He *wanted* you to see it. Up to his old tricks again."

Milo? No . . . Milo hadn't done any of the things they'd thought he had, so he couldn't have done this, either. Milo wasn't a criminal. Milo was a victim. *Their* victim, and they would have to make it up to him somehow.

But . . . if Milo was innocent, then who . . . who was *guilty*?

And why was Trucker lying about Milo?

Then she watched, lost in confusion, as Trucker waded into the water and bent to remove the photograph. And as he stretched out his arm, the collar of his shirt gaped open further and revealed a cruel, jagged slash in the soft flesh of his throat. It looked painful. And it looked recent. As recent as, say, no more than a week ago?

When she slashed backward with that chunk of glass, toward a figure straddling her and leaning forward to whisper in her ear, where would her thrusting arm have been likeliest to strike? The face . . . or the throat? There was no mark on Trucker's face. But there *was* a very ugly mark, the kind easily made by a large chunk of broken glass, on his throat.

She had begun backing away even before he stood up, saying, "I think I'll leave it there. It's proof that Milo hated Giselle. We can show the others when they get home. When I tell them I saw Milo put it there . . ." his voice broke off as he saw the expression on her face.

She realized, too late, that she should have hidden the fact that she'd guessed the truth. Maybe she would have had a chance, then. He knew the minute he looked at her. She could see it in his eyes.

"Where is Ian?" she whispered. "What have you done to him?"

Chapter 27

Trucker laughed. "You could say Ian's . . . *tied up* right now." Seeing the look of horror on her face, he added, "Oh, relax. He's still breathing. And he never knew what hit him."

Ian was okay. Jess began to breathe again. But . . . he wouldn't be able to help her out of this.

Her eyes moved to the photograph, still flapping in the water. "You . . . *you* killed Giselle?"

Trucker's expression sobered. "I didn't mean to. I didn't want to. It was *her* fault." His eyes darkened with rage. "She made me so mad. The way she treated me, after all I'd done for her."

Jess wanted to turn and run. But there was nowhere close by to run to. Trucker would catch up with her . . . and kill her.

Jess kept her voice level. "What had you done

for her, Trucker?" If she could keep him talking, stall till the others got home . . .

Trucker's face took on a faraway look, and his voice softened. "Her car broke down on the freeway one afternoon. It was raining, I remember, a real summer downpour. I was driving a tow truck to earn some money for college, and my truck was the first one to come along. When I knocked on her window, she rolled it down, and then she started crying. I mean, it was a cloudburst. I could tell she wasn't the kind of person who cried all the time, and this had been building up for a while. The dam just burst. She spilled out all this stuff about her mom being in the hospital, really sick, and her dad not being home when she tried to call him from one of the freeway phones and how she hadn't wanted the stupid little sports car in the first place. She said her daddy only gave it to her because he felt guilty about spending so much time at the hospital."

Trucker shook his head, not noticing that Jess was shuffling her feet backward in the tiniest of steps as he spoke. "At first, I thought she was just some spoiled rich girl. But the more she talked, the more I could see she needed taking care of. So," he finished proudly, "that's what I did. I took her home, got her car fixed, and when I brought it back to her, I stayed. She was glad to have the company."

"I'm sure she was," Jess agreed, nodding.

"And I never left her side again, except to go to work, the rest of the summer. I could see that her old friends didn't understand her like I did. They weren't what she needed. *I* was all she needed. After a while, she saw that, too. She didn't need anybody but me. That made us both happy."

Suddenly, Trucker shouted, "Stop right there! And don't move another step!" His face twisted in anger. "You must think I'm a complete idiot!" Thrusting the still lit flashlight into a front pocket of his jeans, which turned his face into an eerie yellow mask, he reached into another pocket and pulled out a long, thin wire, bending it into a circle.

Like a necklace, Jess thought, her heart pounding.

Keep him talking, her mind warned fiercely. "If you were so good to Giselle," she said rapidly, "why didn't she go with you when you came here to get her last spring?"

He had begun walking toward her slowly, the

wire held loosely in his hands. Her question stopped him. His eyes narrowed. "Because this place changed her." He glanced up the hill toward Nightingale Hall, its lights gleaming faintly through the trees. His voice shook with rage. "I *hate* this place!"

But when he looked at Jess again, he spoke normally. "That summer, she *agreed* when I said we'd be together forever. But then her mother died and her father remembered that he had a daughter. Giselle was so grateful for the attention he finally gave her that she agreed to go to college when he insisted. She didn't *want* to. She didn't want to leave me, I know she didn't. She did it for him."

Jess didn't believe that. Maybe Trucker honestly believed that, or maybe he was just kidding himself. But from everything she'd heard about Giselle, she believed college had always been in Giselle's plans. A momentary loneliness and terrible sense of loss had made her temporarily dependent upon Trucker. That was understandable. But Jess was certain that even if Giselle's father hadn't pulled himself out of his grief and tended to his daughter again, sooner or later Giselle would have ended her dependence on Trucker. In fact, going off to college had probably been her first step in that direction.

And Jess would bet anything that Giselle had left willingly, maybe even eagerly. She had probably never *intended* to marry Trucker. He'd wanted it so much, he'd fantasized that it was true.

"Then she came *here*," Trucker went on, delivering another glowering stare toward the house. "And she changed. She ignored my phone calls, my letters. I thought we'd get it all straightened out at Christmas. But she didn't come *home*. She went to stay with a friend instead." His eyes went back to Jess. "She was so ungrateful! After everything I'd *done* for her!"

Jess's ears strained for the distant sound of tires on gravel. But the air remained maddeningly still. An owl hooted up near the house, but there was no crunching of gravel.

"You did all that stuff in the house," Jess said, "and framed Milo. Why? No one even knew Giselle had been . . . killed. Or that you had anything to do with her death."

"Sooner or later, someone would have found the letters and asked some questions. I knew they were here, so I came here, got a job, and started hunting. When Milo showed up, I knew I had the perfect patsy for a frame, because he'd known Giselle. She talked about him a lot. She felt bad because they weren't friends anymore. As soon as I heard his name that first day on the front porch, I knew I was home free. How many guys named Milo can there be? Just to be sure, I asked him where he was from, and I wasn't disappointed. So I snatched Cath's essay and later planted it in Milo's notebook. And I knew exactly where I'd plant the letters when I did find them. In Milo's room." Trucker grinned. "And it worked, didn't it?"

"But you and Milo were in the cellar together. Didn't he *see* you take the letters?"

"I was down there alone long enough to find the letters before Milo got there."

"And he never sent you upstairs for soda, did he? You were setting him up, letting us know he was down there alone because you were already planning to hide the letters in his room."

"Smart girl. But I didn't have *all* the letters. *You* still had one."

"If you'd killed me in the cellar," Jess said,

her voice shaking, "You *never* would have found the letter I had."

"I intended to blow up the house and everything in it that night," Trucker said, his own voice trembling with fury. "But *you* turned off the gas. You ruined my plan. And now," his voice grew softer again as he began walking toward her, the wire in his hands, "you have to be punished for that. I'll take care of Nightingale Hall and your precious friends later, when they're all asleep in their beds."

"They'll come looking for me," she protested, beginning to back away again. "They won't go to bed if I'm not there."

"Yeah, they will," he said casually. "Because you'll leave a note saying you and Ian have decided to make a night of it elsewhere." He grinned. "They'll believe that, of course, because *Ian* won't be around, either. He'll be here. With you." His voice became cheerful, almost lilting. "I think watery graves are kind of romantic, don't you?"

Jess searched wildly for another question and found one. "But if you loved her, how could you *kill* her, Trucker?"

His jaw clenched. "She wouldn't come *with* me, stupid! I came all this way and then she said she didn't *love* me, which I *knew* wasn't true. It was this *place*, the people she lived with here, that turned her against me. I knew if she'd just come away with me and we were alone together, we'd get back to where we used to be. But she was so *stubborn*." Trucker shook his head. "It wasn't my fault. She *made* me lose my temper!"

"You strangled her and made it look like suicide."

Trucker frowned. "Well, of *course* I made it look like suicide. What choice did I have?" And then, his eyes shining yellow like a wild animal's in the glow of the flashlight in his pocket, he advanced upon her, the nasty-looking wire held out in front of him.

Jess knew she couldn't outrun him. She could fight him, but he was heavier, stronger than she was. She had nothing in her hands but her high heels and although she glanced around frantically, she saw nothing she could use as a weapon.

Trembling violently with fear and frustration, she threw her heels at him. They bounced harmlessly off his chest and fell to the ground.

Trucker laughed and kept advancing.

When she tried later to explain what happened next, no matter how carefully she put it, it came out wrong. Because there wasn't any way for it to come out *right* and still make sense.

One second, Trucker was almost upon her, the wicked wire necklace in his hands, and she knew she was about to die.

But in the next second, the wet photograph of Giselle ripped free of the rock holding it hostage, lifted itself up out of the babbling creek, and whooshed through the air to plaster itself across Trucker's face. It molded itself to his features like a second skin, blinding him and effectively sealing off his air passages.

As Jess watched with her mouth open, her eyes wide in disbelief, Trucker dropped the wire circle to claw frantically at the sodden, smothering photograph. It remained firmly plastered to his face. His chest heaved in an effort to breathe. His feet staggered backward as he fought to escape the suffocating mask. When he fell, his hands still digging and scraping at the dripping wet picture of Giselle McKendrick forming a death mask over his face, he fell hard, backward, into the creek.

There was a loud, sharp crack as his head crashed into the round, smooth rock that had held the photograph prisoner only moments earlier.

Trucker's feet thrashed in the water once,

and then he lay still. The flashlight in his front jeans pocket cast its eerie yellow glow upward, illuminating, where his face should have been, an eight by ten glossy photograph of a beautiful blonde girl with bright blue eyes.

She was smiling.

Chapter 28

Her eyes fixed on the photograph smiling up at her from Trucker's lifeless body, Jess sank to her knees. "Thank you," she whispered, "thank you, Giselle."

A hand on her shoulder caused her to jump.

"Take it easy," a voice behind her said. Ian bent to peer into her face. "You okay?" A streak of dried blood made a dark red circle on his forehead.

Speechless, she nodded. Footsteps crunched on the other side of her. When she looked up, Milo was standing there. Cath, Jon, and Linda, still in their Ball clothes, were behind him, their faces white with shock.

She hadn't heard the crunch of tires on gravel.

"Oh, Milo," Jess cried, "you came back! I'm so sorry we accused you."

"It's okay." Milo knelt beside her. They all stared at the bizarre scene in the creek. "I knew it was him," he said of Trucker. "We were the only two in the cellar with that trunk. I knew *I* hadn't taken the letters. So last week, I went back home to do some investigating. When I described Trucker to Giselle's father, he said it sounded exactly like the guy Giselle had been dating, who'd said his name was Brandon. McKendrick didn't like the guy at all. He said he'd taken too much control over Giselle's life at a time when she was especially vulnerable. Her father blames himself. Said if he'd been paying more attention . . ."

"But his wife was dying," Jess murmured.

"Right. The only person to blame is Trucker." Milo and Ian helped Jess to her feet. "I came back to straighten things out. But when I went upstairs, I heard Ian trying to break down the closet door with his feet. I'd just let him out when everyone else came home. You were the only one missing, Jess. And then Ian looked out an upstairs window and spotted the flashlight down at the creek."

"Let's get out of here," Ian said, and Jess nodded numbly.

And then, just as they turned to leave, there was a sudden gust of wind. The soft whisper of wet paper pulled their attention back to the creek. They watched in shocked silence as Giselle's photograph slowly peeled itself away from Trucker's face, lifted itself up, and flew swiftly through the air, up the creekbed until it was out of sight.

When Jess could find her voice, she whispered, almost to herself, "She put the shadow on my wall, too, and the footprints in the hall leading to my room. She was trying to tell me . . ."

"What?" Ian asked. "What are you talking about?"

Jess smiled wearily. "Nothing. Never mind." But silently, she added, " 'Bye, Giselle. Rest in peace."

Together, they all climbed back up the hill in silence, Ian holding Jess's hand. When they reached the clearing behind Nightingale Hall, something in the air . . . a sudden, hushed stillness, stopped them in their tracks. They lifted their heads and listened.

And as they stood there, the big old brick house seemed to shudder, as if sighing heavily, and then settle back on its haunches peacefully.

When the air was still again, Milo said, "Giselle found justice, and the house is satisfied. It isn't waiting anymore."

No one laughed.

"Come on," Jess said quietly. "We can go inside now."

About the Author

"Writing tales of horror makes it hard to convince people that I'm a nice, gentle person," says Diane Hoh.

"So what's a nice woman like me doing scaring people?

"Discovering the fearful side of life: what makes the heart pound, the adrenaline flow, the breath catch in the throat. And hoping always that the reader is having a frightfully good time, too."

Diane Hoh grew up in Warren, Pennsylvania. Since then, she has lived in New York, Colorado, and North Carolina, before settling in Austin, Texas. "Reading and writing take up most of my life," says Hoh, "along with family, music, and gardening." Her other horror novels include *Funhouse, The Accident, The Invitation, The Fever*, and *The Train*.

Killers, vampires, aliens, ghosts. Learn the true meaning of fear.